HIGH STAKES AT HOOPFEST

Also by Chris Bieker

Murder at Manito

Blood on Bloomsday

HIGH STAKES
AT
HOOPFEST

A Rex Begonia Mystery

Chris Bieker

High Stakes at Hoopfest

Cover Art by Megan Perkins © 2024, All rights reserved.
Book design by Russel Davis, Gray Dog Press

Print Edition ISBN: 978-1-7352191-4-1
Digital Edition ISBN: 978-1-7352191-5-8

Printed in the United States of America

*for Meaghan
the sunflower in my garden*

Chapter 1

A TURN FOR THE WORSE

Tuesday Evening

Ivy felt content. After a grueling day of finishing up reports for her job as a junior detective on the Spokane Police homicide unit, she leaned against her boyfriend Beau Hunter. From their perch on the basalt overlook at Palisades Park, they watched the fading light of the orange and violet sunset reflect off the Lilac City's buildings a few miles northeast of where they sat. Stars began to illuminate the sky above them as the city lights twinkled below among the sprawling metropolis on the horizon.

Beau's strong arm wrapped around Ivy's shoulder and she caught a whiff of his warm skin with a hint of Husky as the evening breeze blew wisps of her flaming-red hair across her face. She reached up to pull the stray locks back in place and felt her arm nudged by Beau's dog Yukon, who insisted on wriggling in between them.

Ivy reached over to scratch Yukon behind the ears and put her face to his. "How can a girl resist those bright, starlit blue eyes?" she asked.

"How about by looking into a pair of deep brown eyes?" teased Beau, feeling slightly neglected.

Headlights from the nearby road cut through the increasing darkness as the sound of a speeding car interrupted the quiet, peaceful evening. It's traveling much too fast for that windy road, thought Ivy. She recalled the 15-miles per hour warning signs with squiggly arrows every 100 yards or so.

A moment later, she heard the squeal of brakes followed by a horrifying crash. The thud of a car coming to a forced stop and the sound of metal crunching brought Ivy and Beau to their feet. They rushed toward the road. Yukon yipped and scrambled after them.

They stopped at Beau's pickup, in the parking area, just long enough to grab a flashlight and first-aid kit. Always prepared — there are advantages to dating an overgrown Boy Scout thought Ivy, smiling momentarily.

The beam from the flashlight helped them pick their way down the hill and through the brush toward where headlights glared silently. The pair stopped where the woods met the road. A giant ponderosa pine had halted the trajectory of a cherry-red Ferrari. The front end of the car resembled an accordion and the windshield sported a spider web of cracks.

Beau directed the flashlight beam through the cracked glass. Vacant eyes on a bloody, pallid face stared back at Beau and Ivy. What must have been a handsome middle-aged man now appeared battered and bloodied, his rumpled but expensive looking suit twisted haphazardly on the marred body.

"Looks like his evening took a turn for the worse. We're going to need help," said Beau.

Ivy stifled a gag. Then, she immediately dialed 9-1-1 as Beau yanked at the car door. Initially, the mangled metal impeded his efforts.

"Send an ambulance quickly. There's been a terrible crash," Ivy pleaded. "A man's been hurt. He's bleeding and unconscious. I don't know if we can get to him in the car. It's so banged up." She meant the car but the statement could apply equally to the man inside.

Despite working for the homicide unit for the past three years and seeing her share of bodies, Ivy still sounded frantic after having the gruesome scene interrupt their serene evening. She calmed down long enough to give the dispatcher a description of their location and her phone number before turning her attention to helping Beau.

Whether due to hinges coming loose during the crash or the adrenaline-enhanced efforts of Beau and Ivy, the car door finally popped off the vehicle, throwing the two rescuers to the ground. The body slumped out on top of them.

"Augh!" yelled Beau as he let go of the door and rolled aside.

Ivy scrambled to her feet and then back toward the body, now sprawled on the ground. She checked for a pulse and leaned in toward the bloodied face to listen for breathing. Whew! The man smelled like a whiskey distillery! No antiseptic needed here. Wait! Did she detect faint breathing? It only lasted a few seconds and then stopped.

"He's alive! But barely," she blurted out. Without hesitation, she reached over his chest and began compressions. "Come on, stay with me." She started quietly singing, "…staying alive…staying alive… " And then, "Breathe!"

Beau retrieved the first-aid kit from where he had set it down and pulled out latex gloves and gauze. He attempted to stem the bleeding from the man's head.

Ivy knew the man's survival depended on them responding quickly, but time seemed to stop. All she could see was the bloody, pale face and smell the alcohol. All she could hear was her own singing as she pumped. She knew Beau was there bandaging the man and treating for shock while Yukon valiantly stood guard in the dark.

Finally, a faint sound of sirens grew louder. And then a fire truck, followed by an ambulance and a patrol car, pulled to a stop along the road. Emergency Medical Technicians relieved Ivy and Beau from their rescue efforts and loaded the injured man into the ambulance to take him to Holy Heart Hospital.

"If this guy lives, he owes you," the lead EMT declared. "You both did a fine job tending to him."

Before leaving the scene, the EMTs checked for the injured man's identification and shared the information with the responding police officer, Stan Silva.

"Looks like a DUI, officer," said one of the EMTs. "You know what they say — drinking and driving don't mix. That's especially true on *this* road!"

Silva agreed and promised to follow up later at the hospital after interviewing Ivy and Beau.

"What brings you out here tonight?" Silva asked, turning to Ivy and her partner after they had a chance to catch their breath and let the adrenaline settle.

Ivy felt herself blush. She then hurriedly launched into recounting the evening's excitement to Officer Silva, a colleague with the Spokane

Police Department. She skipped over the romantic details from earlier in the evening. Those she would save for her personal diary. It had taken Ivy years and the successful resolution of criminal cases to earn the respect of her male colleagues. She wanted to maintain a professional persona.

"Sounds like the guy was lucky you were nearby," Silva observed wryly, after Ivy finished her chronology of events.

"Yeah, we haven't had time to get together for weeks. We finally had an evening to ourselves. And then this. I wonder who he is?" Beau asked, not noticing Silva's wink. "He was driving a pretty fancy car. You don't often see Ferraris in Spokane."

"According to his driver's license, he's from Las Vegas," Silva explained. "Name's Tip Seeborn. I'll stop by Holy Heart and see how Seeborn's doing and give you an update in the office tomorrow," he added, being serious and turning toward Ivy.

"Thanks." Ivy couldn't shake the vision of Seeborn's gruesome face and hoped that he would be okay. She was tired. She and Beau headed back toward the truck with Yukon scampering behind them. At least her diary entry tonight would be more exciting than the police reports she slogged through earlier in the day.

Chapter 2

HOOPTOWN, U.S.A.

Wednesday

When Ivy walked into the Spokane Police headquarters break room early the next morning, she almost bumped into Detective Rex Begonia. Spokane's senior homicide investigator, Rex was Ivy's partner and mentor in the department. He had served there nearly 25 years when the new young officer had burst onto the scene. It was only after solving a number of cases together that the perky, outgoing Ivy finally won over the reserved older detective.

"Sorry, Boss," said Ivy rubbing her eyes. "I didn't sleep too well last night. Bad dreams."

"Dreams about car wrecks? I heard a DUI crashed your date last night," Rex said while meticulously measuring finely ground beans into his personal espresso machine. "Maybe you should switch up the tea and try something stronger this morning." He handed her a cup of his specially made espresso.

"Thanks, Boss." Ivy took a sip and scrunched her petite nose at the bitterness. "Now I know why this stuff is served in tiny cups."

Rex looked offended. Obviously, he still had much to teach Ivy.

His expression didn't register with Ivy, who was still distracted. "Yeah, not how I imagined the evening ending," she said. "It seems like every time Beau and I have a romantic date planned, something happens to ruin it — a lowlife cuts down his partner and next thing you know, I'm working on a murder case. Or, Beau gets called to capture a moose loose in Manito Park. It's always something.

"Guess I should be thankful though. The poor guy in the car had a worse ending to his night. I saw on KRUM-TV news this morning that he didn't make it," Ivy continued. She appeared downcast. Her CPR efforts had been Herculean, but obviously not enough to keep the man alive.

"Hey, it wasn't your fault," Rex attempted to reassure his partner after registering her expression. "I heard from Silva that the guy suffered from traumatic head injury. He really didn't stand a chance."

"Did Silva say anything else? Did he find out any details about who the guy was, or why he was speeding on the windy road after dark?"

"The man's family hasn't been notified yet, but after they have, the media will blow up with the news," Rex responded. "Tip Seeborn was Mayor Prosciutto's campaign manager. He had just left a fundraising party at the home of Wes Larch — remember that developer we questioned in the Manito Case a couple of years ago?"

In addition to being a suspect in the death of his business partner, the shady Larch had been involved in dirty land dealings which harmed small-acreage farmers. His latest scheme entailed a contract with the city to upgrade a section of Riverfront Park and build a 10,000 square-foot professional grade basketball court to debut during Hoopfest, an upcoming basketball tournament. The mayor's critics claimed Larch landed the lucrative city contract because of his financial support for Mayor Prosciutto's gubernatorial campaign.

Mayor Sammy Prosciutto had his detractors but he did enjoy a level of popularity most previous Spokane mayors never experienced. This was due to his success keeping the potholes in the roads filled and the priority he placed on parks. Spokanites were passionate about their parks and green spaces.

Of course, it helped that one brother in the mayor's huge Italian-American family owned the largest concrete and asphalt company in the area. Three of the mayor's other siblings held high-level positions with the city. But having an Italian heritage and the beneficial family connections also meant that the mayor constantly refuted rumors of nepotism and mafia connections.

Now, Mayor Prosciutto had set his eyes on the open governor's seat. He hoped to be the first governor elected from Eastern Washington in decades. After all, he knew how to get out the green vote and this *was* the Evergreen State.

Rex, who shared an Italian-American heritage with the city's top official, sympathized with Mayor Prosciutto's sensitivity to stereotypes. However, the mayor did fit one stereotype, thought Rex. He could be hot-tempered. The mayor would seethe at the media attention garnered by the death of his campaign manager. The fact that Tip Seeborn had been drinking heavily and coming from a campaign fundraiser hosted by Wes Larch only made matters worse. Looks like trouble for the mayor, surmised Rex.

"Ooh, I'd hate to be the mayor's PR person," Ivy quipped.

"Me too," echoed Officer Stan Silva as he entered the break room. He drained the dregs from the communal coffee pot and grabbed a jelly doughnut from the ever present plate of pastries on the table. He ignored Rex's disapproving look as he dipped the doughnut in the coffee. "The mayor's asked Chief Blueblood to order an investigation to see if the vehicle involved in the wreck was intentionally tampered with. Somehow, Prosciutto doesn't believe his campaign manager drank enough at the event to drive his sporty car off a twisty road in the middle of the night."

"Probably just trying to cover his…" Rex started.

"That's enough," said Police Chief Blueblood, walking into the room. "Even if this break room isn't bugged, election season has started and we have to stay above the fray."

Rex reddened. That's why Barney Blueblood was the police chief and Rex stuck with being a homicide detective. Chief Blueblood possessed a political sense that the detective lacked. Friendly and politically astute, Chief Blueblood, a Spokane Indian, was universally beloved in the community and buffered the police force from the fiery mayor. Rex regarded the chief's appointment as one of the mayor's best decisions.

Ivy looked around the room. She'd never considered the possibility of it being bugged. Would Mayor Prosciutto really stoop that low?

"Not only is it election season, but Hoopfest happens in just a week and a half. Attention will be on the city," the chief announced. "There will be more than 250,000 people downtown. We'll need every officer working that weekend."

The chief asked a young woman wearing dreadlocks and sitting near him to stand. "Officer Sativa, here, will take the lead for the undercover narcotics unit. We've had reports that a new drug cartel is trying to elbow its way into Spokane during the basketball games," he said, before adding, "Make sure to check the board for your assignments."

Despite the online assignment board being accessible to the entire department, Chief Blueblood still posted the schedule near the bulletin board in the break room. Never know when the computer might go down or the power goes out, he reasoned.

"Hey, how come O'Dendron's not on the schedule?" asked Silva, looking over the assignments.

"Special dispensation," replied the chief.

Sergeant Phil O'Dendron was Rex's closest friend in the department. The pair had served together for more than two decades. O'Dendron's outgoing and active personality complimented the detective's introverted and contemplative one. The big, burly sergeant was also a former basketball player for Gonzaga University and volunteered as the Division Marshal for Hoopfest's Elite Division. The task would occupy much of his non-work hours for the next week and a half.

Every final full weekend in June for more than 30 years, the Lilac City transformed into Hooptown U.S.A., hosting the world's largest three-on-three basketball tournament and appropriating downtown city streets and part of the city center's Riverfront Park for Hoopfest. More than a quarter million people descended on Spokane to play, volunteer or watch the sporting event that shut down 45 city blocks. Players, young and old, from almost every state in the nation, turned out to make up the more than 6,000 teams vying to be basketball champions.

And it was at this pinnacle event that Mayor Sammy Prosciutto planned to capture statewide voters' attention on his fair city and brandish his leadership proficiency. A possible scandal over an intoxicated campaign manager just would not do.

Chapter 3

FAMILY TIME

Wednesday Evening

Later that evening, Ivy pulled up in her green Volkswagen bug in front of the Begonia family home. The car's characteristic whirling gurgle sound announced her arrival. The bug was old but it still ran like a Swiss clock. She had owned it since high school. The constant maintenance on it helped her bond with her dad, Joe Lizei, with whom she often ate dinner, but who was currently out of town.

As much as she liked and admired Rex, her professional partner and mentor, she really would rather have dined with Beau this evening. He was working late. Again. Then, he and his Hoopfest teammates would play basketball for an hour, practicing for the big event. There wasn't much time for courting during Hoopfest season! She really couldn't fault Beau. Her job as a detective on the homicide unit demanded just as much time as his job as a wildlife officer. And both their schedules could be unpredictable. Crimes in the human and animal worlds didn't exactly follow a nine to five schedule.

She really ought to be thankful to the Begonias for including her in their weekly family meal. Ivy loved being around Rex's large, boisterous Italian-American family. Four or five conversations always seemed to occur simultaneously, a contrast with the serene dinners she shared with her own father. This was one of those evenings she craved being surrounded by people. Rex had invited her to join the Begonia gathering when he realized her dinner date had fallen through. He really could be like an older brother sometimes.

Ivy grabbed the bottle of Sangiovese she had brought on a recommendation from a nearby wine shop and stepped out of the car.

As she climbed the steps to the wrap-around porch, the front door of the two-story home burst open and a petite woman with long, wavy, jet-black hair rushed out, stretching her arms wide to embrace Ivy.

"Benvenuto," exclaimed a smiling Sophie.

Rex's youngest sister, Sophie, was the sibling whose company Ivy most enjoyed.

"Thanks," she said accepting the bottle of wine Ivy held out to her. "My brother told me you would be joining us tonight. I'm so happy you are here, Ivy. Martina and Nobu are helping Mama in the kitchen and everyone else is playing basketball. I'm sooooo bored! Let's pour a big glass of vino, sit out on the porch and talk." And then as if an afterthought, she added jokingly, "Unless you want to play basketball."

"Kidding, right?" laughed four-foot ten-inch Ivy.

The two women went inside where the scent of Bolognese sauce simmering triggered Ivy's appetite. Mama Begonia wrapped her in a welcoming hug and Ivy immediately felt part of the family. Sophie's husband, the famous chef Nobu Hiyamugi, offered her a pre-dinner bruschetta while Sophie filled two large glasses with wine. Handing one to Ivy, she pulled her guest by the arm out to a table and chairs on the back porch. "Now, I want to hear all about that handsome wildlife officer of yours."

"Oh Sophie, I just don't know," Ivy sighed as they sat at the table overlooking the driveway where a multi-generational Begonia basketball game was in full play. "We had our first fight. Can you believe we fought about not spending enough time together? I really like being with Beau but we hardly ever see each other. I don't even know if I could pick him out in a line up!

"It's like we're both married to our jobs," she continued. "I mean, I'm not complaining about my job. The last few years have been great. I've helped solve some major cases. And now when the guys tease me, it's in fun. Not like in the beginning when it felt like hazing. I've gained confidence and the chief and my co-workers have noticed my efforts. Your brother has even talked with me about a possible promotion. But then I'd be even busier! How will I ever have time for a serious relationship? How do you and Nobu manage? You both have crazy, busy careers."

"Well don't let my brother mentor you on relationships. He's a self-proclaimed, lifetime hermit," Sophie laughed. Sophie Begonia was a lawyer, helping women leave domestic violence situations. Her husband Nobu owned and operated the Fusion Noodle Bistro and hosted a cooking show on KRUM-TV. They had been married for eleven years.

"First, take a breath. Or better yet, take a long sip of this nice Sangiovese you brought. Now swirl it around in your mouth."

Ivy did. Flavors of cherry and plum exploded in her mouth. She wasn't sure what it had to do with her relationship with Beau but she did feel the stress ease from her body.

"Do you taste the intricate flavors? When the wine is young it can be highly acidic, so not so tasty. But as it ages… Ah, the best Sangiovese wines are complex and long-lasting — like the best relationships."

Ivy silently congratulated herself for requesting a recommendation at the wine shop. "Your marriage is like Sangiovese?" she asked quizzically. "Or does drinking lots of wine keep you married longer?"

"Maybe both," laughed Sophie. "Really, you just have to relax and trust that it will all work out in the long run. Relationships have their ups and downs but if you just keep at it, your relationship will develop like a smooth, fine wine."

Ivy's dad often shared advice with her in the form of metaphors and stories, also. Joe Lizei worked hard to raise her after her mom died when Ivy was twelve. With the help of his own father, Joe managed the family plant nursery and cared for his daughter. She loved and appreciated him so much but it was also comforting to receive advice from a female friend. And, Italians really do know a thing or two about living well she thought as she sank further back in her chair and took another long sip of the deep red wine.

Suddenly, both women were jarred from their tête-à-tête by a loose basketball that crashed into the porch railing. A loud disagreement followed between 17-year old Tony and 18-year old Giovanni Begonia at the nearby basketball hoop.

"Foul!"

"No way!"

"Yes, way. It was flagrant!"

Gabriella, Mia and Lucia stopped and rolled their eyes while waiting for their male cousins to finish arguing.

"Ha," said Sophie as the two women watched the players. "Sports brings out the testosterone in males. It gives them a chance to show off in front of us females."

"Based on Beau's descriptions of wildlife mating rituals, humans aren't all that different," Ivy admitted.

Just then, Rex's oldest sister, Martina opened the door and called out for everyone to come in for supper. As the clan streamed up the porch steps, Ivy noticed Rex trying not to appear hobbling. He couldn't hide it successfully. She didn't want to ask about it in front of everyone else, so she decided to wait.

The evening stretched into the late hours as the Begonia family and Ivy reveled in a spicy spaghetti Bolognese dinner topped off with animated conversation — much of it on the fine points of politics, the produce business or competitive basketball.

When the evening came to a close, Ivy offered to drop Rex off at his home. He agreed but expressed doubts about her old bug making it up the steep South Hill. The car was almost as old as he was!

"Ah come on, Boss. Not a problem. Even when new, Volkswagons sound like they're going to fall apart. This one's in great shape. Pop and I care for it like it's a baby. It's a classic!"

As he bent his aching, aging knees to get into the small car, Rex wondered whether he, too, was a classic. Or was he just an oldster?

Chapter 4

HIGH PRESSURE

Wednesday Night

After a hot shower, Rex placed ice packs on his knees and felt grateful he wouldn't be competing in Hoopfest. He was happy enough to play against family members in pickup games. He plopped into the comfort of his favorite overstuffed chair, a trusty companion of many years. His legs stretched before him while a fan in the window created a mild breeze. Books — as diverse as *The Biology of Plants* to *The Complete Collection of Sherlock Holmes* — covered an entire wall of shelves, as they competed with the number of plants in the room. Except for the aching knees, it was a perfect end to the evening, thought Rex as he sipped an espresso heavily laced with Frangelico and turned on the nightly news.

On screen, KRUM-TV reporter Molly Murrow interviewed Manito Park's Head Gardener Toni Fritts about a disaster that had befallen the park's beloved Duncan Garden. The story caught Rex's attention, due as much to the attractive reporter as to the topic of the story.

He and Molly had resumed a romantic relationship after many years apart. They dated in college when he majored in criminal justice and she studied journalism and communications at Gonzaga University. But then Molly left for the big time and became a celebrity investigative reporter across the state in Seattle and Rex didn't have the heart to hold her back. Besides, he wasn't sure an investigative reporter was a good match for a private person like himself. While in Seattle, Molly married a big tech CEO and later divorced him. Rex remained single. Had life passed him by while he concentrated on his career? he wondered.

After 18 years in Seattle, Molly had returned to Spokane. "I missed the sense of community," she had said. Rex hoped that wasn't all she missed.

In the past few months, they began to date again. Since taking on extroverted Ivy as a partner and mentee, Rex began to slowly emerge from his hermit shell and engage more with others on a personal basis. Now, he and Molly regularly met for dinner at the Fusion Noodle Bistro or at O'Donovan's Pub for drinks whenever their busy schedules allowed. He always felt ten years younger when he was with Molly. Her intelligence and curious mind had always attracted Rex. Now, he watched the television as Molly turned that inquisitiveness toward the story about the mystery of plants dying in Manito's gardens.

"We don't know what caused the stunted and deformed growth of many of the annual plants in the gardens," Head Gardener Toni Fritts told Molly. She held up a discolored, twisted lupine as an example. "We've collected samples and sent them to the labs at Washington State University but it's going to take awhile to get the results. Meanwhile, park visitors are complaining loudly about all these empty flower beds. We had to dig them out and add more soil. It's a bit of a mess at the moment."

"Will the gardens be ready to receive the many expected visitors to Spokane during Hoopfest weekend?" asked Molly. Manito Park attracted many a Lilac City visitor, even the sporting kind. "And isn't the Art in the Park event that same weekend?"

"We'll have to rely on the goodwill and efforts of Spokane's garden club volunteers to help park staff replant the beds," answered Fritts. "Fortunately, Spokane abounds with big-hearted gardeners. We'll be ready."

The news switched to the weather. Forecaster Misty Mourne predicted, "The rest of the week will be rainy and cold, keeping with tradition for the week following the end of school. A high pressure system will move in by next week and temperatures will start heating up…"

A commercial for Mort Short's Sporting Goods store came on the screen. The store had a special on basketball shoes. A campaign ad for Sammy Prosciutto followed. It showed the mayor in Riverfront Park and highlighted his support for parks and open spaces. It also extolled his record on fighting crime — thanks to the Spokane Police, thought Rex — and his competence running the Lilac City. This made him the best candidate for Governor of the Evergreen State, according to the ad.

The news resumed with sportscaster Duncan Wilson interviewing current and former Gonzaga University basketball standouts who planned to play in the elite division at Hoopfest. Thanks to the Bulldogs' success at the national level, many Americans now could pronounce correctly Gonzaga (Gone-zag-ah) and Spokane (Spo-can)!

Keeping with the Hoopfest theme, the cameras turned to an interview with Hal Hoozer, Hoopfest Director. The reporter asked Hoozer if downtown would be ready in time for the games given that a perpetual state of construction closed many of the main streets in the heart of the city.

"Well now, that's a question for Mayor Sammy Prosciutto," replied Hoozer. "The new 10,000 square-foot basketball court in Riverfront Park is completed. And, I have it on excellent authority that the streets and all of downtown will be more than ready by the last weekend in June. If the mayor wants the job done, the job will get done — that's the kind of guy he is."

Wow, maybe Hoozer should be in a campaign commercial, thought Rex. He had to give Prosciutto credit for being effective. Prosciutto was the first mayor in decades to get a handle on the city's annual pothole problem. And he did hire Barney Blueblood as his Chief of Police.

Chief Blueblood was a straight arrow and had a natural ability to cushion his officers and detectives from the demanding mayor. For that, Rex was grateful. The mayor might be capable, but he could be difficult to work with.

The cameras shifted back to the KRUM-TV news room where the anchor gave an update on the death of the mayor's campaign manager, Tip Seeborn. An initial investigation found no foul play involved in Seeborn's death. Mayor Prosciutto had already announced there would be a nationwide search for a new campaign manager.

Rex turned off the television and readied for bed. As usual, he picked up a book to read a chapter before falling asleep. As he replaced a bookmark between the pages of Nathanial Hawthorne's *Rappacini's Daughter,* the phone rang.

Who would call this late? he wondered. Probably the police dispatcher reporting a murder. That might shoot the mayor's record on crime. He picked up the phone, expecting to be called out on a case.

A harried voice on the other end said, "Rex, it's Rugula…"

"How'd you get my home number?"

"No time. I'm working on a story. In danger. They want to kill me to keep me from publishing…"

"What? Who are they? Where are you?"

Too late. The phone line went dead.

Chapter 5

MISSING

Thursday

Rex arrived at the Spokane Police headquarters early the next morning. After dispatching an All Points Bulletin for Arthur Rugula and collecting as much information as he could find on the man late last night, the detective decided to start the search fresh. First up — a strong cappuccino made with his own specialty coffee beans. The watery liquid in the communal coffee pot just disgusted him.

Arthur Rugula was the garden reporter for the local newspaper, the *Spokane Lede*. Single and with no family in the area that Rex knew of, Rugula lived for his job and his love of plants. He had a bit of an acrid personality but had cooperated with detectives during a murder case a few years ago.

After Rugula's cryptic call last night, Rex reached out to the *Spokane Lede* editor Woody Bernstein to determine if the garden reporter's boss knew of Rugula's whereabouts or could provide any details about the reporter's current story. Bernstein hadn't seen Rugula for the past three days. Rugula was easy to overlook. Besides, reporters worked independently for the most part, Bernstein had explained. He did, however, admit a call to the police might be due, so he appreciated Rex notifying him.

As the espresso machine hissed and the dark liquid trickled into Rex's cup, Chief Blueblood walked into the break room. He emptied the last of the communal coffee slop into his mug. Rex watched and winced.

"Good Morning, Rex. Any lunch plans today?"

Rex always planned on lunch. "Did you have something in mind, Chief?" he asked.

"The mayor's making a press announcement at noon today at the Garden of Olives. He's naming an interim campaign manager until the nationwide search can be completed. Thought we might observe. Stay out of the political spotlight, of course. But, it could be interesting to see who's there."

The medical examiner's report showed the mayor's first campaign manager died from wounds sustained during the car wreck, and a blood alcohol level of 0.13 percent in his body likely led to the crash. Did the chief still suspect foul play? wondered Rex.

"Do you think there's more to Tip Seeborn's death than a DUI?" Rex asked the chief.

"No. Just figure it's a good idea to be on guard," responded the chief, absentmindedly filling the empty coffee pot with grounds and water.

"Okay. What time do you want to leave? I'd like to stop by the reporter Arthur Rugula's place this morning to do a wellness check. His editor just filed a missing person's report. Rugula hasn't shown up at the newspaper for the past three days," said Rex. "And, I received an odd call from him last night. He sounded scared. He claimed to be receiving death threats related to some story he was working on but the phone went dead before we ended the conversation."

"He called you at home? That is odd. I didn't even know you were friends. Go ahead. If you aren't back at the office by eleven, I'll just go to the Garden of Olives without you. No worries."

Rex realized that others thought of him as a hermit, but was it implausible that he would receive a phone call at home? "Yeah. I'd like to poke around. See if anything looks suspicious. I can meet you at the restaurant when I'm done."

Thirty minutes later, Rex and Ivy found themselves outside Arthur Rugula's home. The small, brick craftsman was located a few blocks west of Manito Park. Carefully tended roses lined the winding path to the front steps and rounded yellow door. Newspapers piled on the porch and closed shades made the house look unoccupied. Rex tried the door. It was locked.

They made their way around to the back of the house, where an elderly neighbor emptying her garbage into a bin watched them suspiciously from her yard. Rex didn't like the look of a broken glass pane above the back doorknob. He knocked and yelled loudly, "Police. Open up."

No answer. No sounds either.

The elderly woman shuffled toward them. "So you're the police are you?" she asked in a snippety manner. She looked Ivy up and down — all four feet, ten inches — then turned to Rex and said, "I could have used you around here last week when those young whippersnappers were shooting pellet guns at the cute little squirrels."

"Seriously?!" exclaimed Ivy. Who were the criminals here — the neighborhood kids on their way to being thugs, or the robber rodents? If they were like the gray squirrels plaguing Ivy's garden, she chose the squirrels. Gray squirrels weren't even native to the area, according to Beau. And he would know. He worked for the Department of Fish and Wildlife.

"Actually, we're looking for Mr. Rugula," Ivy said, after taking a deep breath. "Do you know him? Have you seen him around here lately?"

"Arthur? Why yes, I do know Arthur. He's a fine neighbor, always helping me with my flowers and yard. Now that you mention it, I haven't seen him for a few days. It's not like him to be absent from his yard this time of the year." The woman began to sound worried.

"When was the last time you saw him?" asked Rex.

"Let's see. He gave me some greens for a salad last Monday and asked me to mail a package for him. Yes, that's the last time I saw him. Oh dear. You don't think something has happened to him, do you?"

"We don't know. That's what we're trying to find out," answered Ivy. "Have you seen or heard anything else that's unusual around here lately?"

"Only the whippersnappers shooting squirrels."

"Here's my card. If you see or hear anything, let us know," said Rex. "And what's your name?"

"Shirley. And that's Arthur's cat Pepper," she said, pointing to a black cat looking frightened and peering out from beneath an Oregon grape bush near Rugula's back door. "Come here Pepper," Shirley called out to the cat.

Rex turned his attention back to the door and called again, "Police. Anyone home?" Nothing. "Time for a wellness check," said Rex.

He tried the door. It wasn't locked. He gently nudged it open and he and Ivy carefully entered the house while Shirley eased back to her own yard where she continued curiously watching the home from afar. The two detectives, with guns drawn, covered each other as they proceeded from room to room. They didn't encounter anyone, but they did find a mess that contradicted the tidiness of the yard. Empty drawers and their contents lay scattered about. Overturned furniture rested upside down. The house appeared as if it had been turned inside out.

"If Rugula was here, he's not now," observed Ivy.

After determining the house unoccupied, Rex put away his gun. "Arthur mentioned he was working on a story. A story that someone didn't want published. Whoever did this was probably looking for whatever information Rugula could use to expose them."

"My guess is they either found it, or it wasn't here. Either way, it would take us days to go through this clutter trying to find who knows what," groused Ivy.

"We need to find Rugula sooner than that. Let's make a cursory scan for anything that might indicate where he might be. I'll call dispatch to send someone to lock the place up as a crime scene. Then we can check back once they finish the report." Rex figured it could take a few days.

It didn't help that Arthur Rugula was as old as Rex. The reporter had five decades to accumulate junk, thought the detective. And judging by these rooms, he kept most of it. They would need a miracle to find a clue.

"What we need is to find his computer," Ivy proclaimed. "Look here, Boss. There's a scanner, router and printer but no computer on his desk. If we find the computer, I bet we solve the case."

Well that was a big if but at least Ivy had the right idea, thought Rex as he returned a catalogue and seed packets from Jenny's Seed Company to the table beside him. He shouldn't be getting distracted.

"Well, let's hope we find it with Rugula. We can't do much more here. We might have just enough time to meet up with the chief and catch the mayor's announcement at the Garden of Olives," said Rex, thinking that if they hurried they might also make it in time for lunch.

Chapter 6

ALL YOU CAN'T EAT

Thursday Afternoon

At the Garden of Olives, Rex and Ivy could barely squeeze past a gaggle of supporters and reporters surrounding Mayor Prosciutto. In a far corner, Chief Blueblood and other top level city employees sat before plates with meal residue. Too late to join the chief for lunch.

Standing before a line of microphones and cameras, Mayor Prosciutto called a tall, lean man with dark, wavy hair and a wide smile to join him. "… I'd like to introduce you to Jake Carville. Jake's my interim campaign manager. He's agreed to come off the bench and coordinate the campaign until I find a permanent replacement.

"Until now, he's done marketing for the campaign. He prefers to remain behind the scenes but rest assured, he's on the ball. He'll get us through this transition time and back in the game. I'm confident we'll be the winning team come November…"

Several reporters broke out into a clamor of questions. Many wanted to know if the mayor could confirm that Tip Seeborn's death had been an accident and asked about the mayor's search for a permanent campaign manager. Then their questions turned toward the readiness of downtown for Hoopfest.

"Citizens are still dodging construction," shouted one reporter. "When will the streets be done?"

One wise guy reporter piped up,"When you're the Governor, will you get the north-south freeway completed so Spokane drivers can avoid the downtown construction congestion?"

Rex could see the red rise in Mayor Prosciutto's neck. Then he heard a familiar voice. Ever the professional, KRUM-TV reporter Molly Murrow brought the conversation back to Jake Carville and the campaign.

"Mayor Prosciutto. Getting back to the campaign, can you tell us how you and Carville will raise your profile outside of the Spokane area? Can you appeal to liberal voters in Western Washington?"

"Excellent question, Molly," responded the mayor, happy for the change in topic. "Washington isn't a red state or a blue state, but a green state. The Evergreen State. Washingtonians care about the outdoors. I have overwhelming support from gardeners, environmentalists, farmers and all outdoor enthusiasts. In fact, Spokane just added a 10,000 square-foot, state of the art basketball court to our crown jewel, Riverfront Park.

"Next week, statewide media attention will be on our city for Hoopfest. It's the largest three-on-three outdoor basketball tournament in the world. I'll be presiding over the festivities. People from all over the state and beyond will see how beautiful and exceptionally managed Spokane is," the mayor emphasized.

Glancing around the room, Rex recognized some of Mayor Prosciutto's supporters. Developer Wes Larch and Judge Rudy Marconi were major donors. Garden club presidents June Bloomenthal and Daisy Denton helped bring in the green vote as well as the greenbacks. City Parks Director Sandy Loamiss and Hoopfest Director Hal Hoozer sat with Chief Blueblood. Rex didn't recognize the other man and woman at the table.

A hostess interrupted his thoughts when she asked Rex and Ivy if they were waiting for a table for lunch. "I'm sorry, we've been so busy this afternoon. We can probably get you a table in another twenty minutes. Or, if you're okay with it, I can seat you at the bar," she told them.

"The bar's fine," replied Ivy, knowing how her partner felt about lunch.

After getting situated with water glasses and menus, Rex ordered the spaghetti Bolognese while Ivy chose ravioli with pesto. After their server left, Rex turned to his partner and said, "I'm not sure what it is, but there's something about that Carville fellow that looks familiar."

"He's not the only one," said Ivy, "Don't look now but there are two guys in the shadows at the end of the bar. I'd swear one of them is Phil Anders, that guy running against Mayor Prosciutto for Governor."

Before Rex could turn around and look, the two men rose and swept past the detectives while heading toward the door. Rex only caught a glimpse of the back of both men. Their casual clothes indicated they weren't in the restaurant to attend the mayor's gathering, not officially anyway.

"Despite the medical examiner's toxicology findings, I'm not ready to concede that there isn't anything suspicious about this election," said Rex, "not where the mayor's concerned."

"What do you find suspicious?" Ivy asked.

"I don't know yet. Something's not right. I've been in this business a long time and my instincts have never failed me."

"Your instincts may be fine," Ivy said, thinking this was a good time to ask about Rex's limp, "But how about your knee? It looked liked it was hurting the other night after the basketball game. Seems like it might have been bothering you again this morning. What's up with the knee?"

"Just a minor setback," responded Rex. He hoped no one had noticed. However, he was touched that Ivy cared. "Just takes longer to bounce back as you get older."

The bartender returned from placing orders with the kitchen. "I'm sorry. We're all out of spaghetti. Apparently, everyone here for the mayor's press conference ordered the all-you-can-eat-spaghetti and we ran out. Can I get you anything else?"

No Rugula, no spaghetti. The day had to improve, thought Rex despairingly.

Chapter 7

A FALLING OUT AND A FALLING OFF

Sunday

Two more days passed without any word from Arthur Rugula and no progress on discovering his whereabouts. The garden reporter still had not shown up at the *Spokane Lede* office. As far as he could tell, Rex was the last person to talk with the missing reporter during the mysteriously truncated phone call the previous week. Rex grew doubtful that Rugula had eluded whatever trouble he faced.

That morning's *Spokane Lede* contained a letter to the editor referencing the mysterious death of garden plants and farm crops in the community. The letter called on the city to investigate and was signed by many of the garden club presidents. Could the issue affect the mayor's support among the garden community? That would be serious.

Speculation about the plant mystery dominated the conversation that evening during a wine tasting event at the Moon Rock Market where Rex had brought Molly on a date. This week's topic — bold, Italian reds had inspired him. Many of the event's attendees lived and gardened in the neighborhood not far from Manito Park. Based on their discussion, anxiety about the garden issue appeared to be growing.

"My lupines are lethargic," lamented a lady in purple who was wolfishly scarfing the salami, "and the monkshood has met its maker. I'll have to replace half the garden!"

"My foxgloves look like they've been poisoned," whined another oenophile.

"My garden club has volunteered to help replant the beds at Manito," offered an elderly gentleman at the end of the table.

24

"I really hoped Ivy and Beau could have joined us tonight," Molly remarked to Rex as they sat across the communal table from each other and compared notes about the wines. She nibbled on a sliver of salty, aged Parmigiano Reggiano and followed it with a sip of Primitivo. "She seems so gregarious. I was looking forward to getting to know your colleague better."

"Ivy said she thought we might have time to get together in a week or two after Hoopfest. I guess when Beau isn't chasing poachers lately, he's preparing for the competition," said Rex. He felt a twinge of envy toward the younger man as he recalled his own limping after the recent pickup b-ball game at the Begonia home. Although, he didn't mind enjoying Molly's company by himself tonight.

Rex knew that with Molly's outgoing and persistent personality, he eventually would have to include her in the rest of his social circle. That could prove difficult since he didn't socialize much beyond family and work. He couldn't imagine his police colleagues warming to an investigative reporter. They much preferred to do the investigating themselves.

Halfway through the evening of sniffing, swirling and sampling the garnet-colored wines, a distant siren interrupted the sommelier extolling a Nebbiolo wine. The sound drew closer. Red and blue lights flashed past the large window behind the spirited wine tasters in the Moon Rock Market.

"Let's go!" Molly grabbed her clutch and was halfway to the door before Rex could catch up with her. They jumped into his classic Fiat 124 and raced in the direction the lights had gone.

They slowed along High Drive, strewn with campaign signs touting Phil Anders, Sammy Prosciutto and the occasional Tammy Hall for Governor. Blazing lights illuminated the faces of a growing crowd along the side of the road. A sense of dread rose in Rex. Could it be an accident? This was a bad place for one. The evening's steady rain had slicked the road. High Drive wound along the top of a bluff with a 500-foot drop-off to Latah Creek below. Few guardrails lined the boulevard. Only the ponderosa pines and brush dotting the steep hillside would catch any vehicle that missed a turn and plunged over the edge.

Rex pulled the Fiat over behind the police cruisers and a fire truck with flashing lights. He and Molly got out and joined the patrol officers at the top of the bluff. An officer kept the growing crowd back from the accident scene.

"What happened, Hollywood?" Rex asked an officer, who appeared to be in charge. It was his colleague, Officer Scott "Hollywood" Pine.

"We have a vehicle over the edge. Two passengers inside. They're banged up pretty badly. Silva and Hemlock are down there now and we've got an ambulance and a tow truck on the way," replied Hollywood. "A neighbor across the street said he heard a large crashing sound. At first, he didn't see anything because of the darkness and drizzle. But, after shining his flashlight across the road, he spotted the mangled end of the guardrail. That's when he knew there'd been an accident."

Officer Silva appeared, climbing up the bluff carrying a stretcher with the help of Officer Hemlock and firefighter EMTs. The scene reminded Rex of Ivy's experience at the Palisades the prior week. Was this another DUI?

"Hey, Rex," Silva acknowledged the detective. "Good to see you here. We could use your help. There's another body down there. We got them both out before the car caught fire but we need some more muscle to get the guy up the hill," said Silva.

Rex secretly smiled about the reference to his muscles in front of Molly. He tossed his Armani jacket to her and slid and scrambled down the hill toward the EMTs struggling to haul another stretcher up the slope. He noticed Silva used the term body. The chances of survival were low, but still... And they wouldn't be the only souls giving it up. The slide down the wet hill spelled doom for his Ferragamo dress shoes.

The officers and EMTs barely managed to get both bodies up the hill before the car's fuel tank exploded, lighting the night sky. The crowd that had gathered along the bluff gasped. Behind the police line, emergency mylar blankets covered the crash victims. By now, the ambulance had arrived and paramedics loaded the first body into the vehicle.

"Didn't even have a chance to do CPR this time," muttered Silva.

Rex didn't comment. Instead, he panted, catching his breath, and looked for Molly. She stood at the edge of the bluff recording events into her phone and photographing the scene. Ever the reporter, he thought.

He turned back toward the remaining shrouded form on the stretcher and pulled back the emergency blanket. A bruised and bloodied face beneath matted, dark wavy hair stared at him.

"OMG, it's the mayor's *new* campaign manager!" exclaimed Molly, who had returned to Rex's side.

It was Jake Carville — Mayor Prosciutto's second campaign manager to die in a car wreck within a week. What are the chances it's a coincidence? thought Rex. Was it vehicular homicide? Did someone cut the brake line? That only happened in movies and television. More likely another DUI. Did the mayor drive his campaign managers to drink? Could the mayor's political opponents be involved?

"You know the family needs to be notified, right?" Rex asked Molly as she furiously noted details from the scene. He quickly realized his mistake.

She glared. "Yes, Rex, I *am* a professional! Of course I know that." She tossed him his jacket and stalked off angrily.

Rex flushed. He wished he could take back his question. Molly had covered numerous police cases in the past and knew the drill. But Carville being the mayor's second campaign manager to die in a car crash within a week was major news. Rex knew the media's desire to publicize information sometimes conflicted with a detective's efforts to build a criminal case. But Molly was right. She had proved her professionalism during many cases in the past.

"Sorry," he muttered to himself. Molly was gone. The apology would have to wait. He had work to do.

Rex turned toward the other officers at the site. "I hope I'm wrong but we need to treat this as if it's a crime scene," he informed them. As the senior officer on the scene, he called the chief to apprise him of the situation, then called dispatch and ordered a full forensic team.

"Where's the witness?" he asked Silva.

As Rex took a statement from the man who had called in the accident, Officer Pine cordoned off the area and sent the responding tow truck driver back to his garage. The firefighters were spraying down the car fire.

The forensic team would need to take measurements and photographs before the remains of the vehicle could be recovered.

A KRUM-TV truck pulled up to the site. Well, that's the end of that date, thought Rex. He and Ivy could commiserate about romantic evenings being cut short by career demands.

Chapter 8

PLANTING A SEED

Monday Morning

Despite staying out late the night before, Rex woke early Monday. He welcomed the morning sun after last night's rain. He called Molly to apologize for questioning her professionalism the prior night but she didn't answer. He left a message and invited her to lunch the next day. That should help make amends, he hoped. He always found good food to be a salve for bruised hearts.

He intended to stop by the post office to pick up a package and enjoy a cup of coffee at Cafe Noir before heading into the office. Ever since the boom in online shopping resulted in an upsurge of porch pirates, he had switched to receiving packages at a post office box. Each new advancement in technology spawned another category of criminals, he theorized. Law enforcement jobs were not in danger of going obsolete!

Yesterday's mail indicated he had a package waiting for him. Also, a few days had gone by since he dropped in at Cafe Noir which, like any respectable coffee shop, opened by 6 a.m. His favorite barista, Gina, probably missed him.

"Hi, Rex," Gina called out flirtatiously when he walked into the cafe with an armload of mail and a newspaper. Rex smiled back and then sat down at his favorite table by the window.

He liked the way the sunlight came through the large window panes and brought out the kaleidoscope of colors in the glass light fixtures and the mosaic tabletops. He set aside the mail and package bound together with a rubber band and picked up the paper to scan the headlines first. Rex believed a good detective needed to stay on top of what was happening in the community.

"This will give you the strength to nab bad guys," Gina said, placing his usual beverage, the Vatican, before him. The hazelnut smell of Frangelico and sweet cardamom wafted up from the cappuccino.

He smiled. At least he was a superhero to someone.

The top story described last night's fiery crash on High Drive that resulted in the death of the mayor's second campaign manager, Jake Carville. The article noted that the Spokane Police Department had not yet determined the cause of the accident. The other body belonged to socialite Jane Moregone, the wife of accountant PJ Moregone. PJ's accounting firm, Moregone Capital, provided financial services for many Spokane businesses, including for Hoopfest. Looking at the newspaper pictures of Carville and Moregone, Rex recognized the woman as one of the two people he couldn't identify at the Garden of Olives. Maybe PJ had been the man seated with her.

Another major story declared street repair downtown was now on the fast track. The Spokane Street Department Director Phil Rhodes predicted completion prior to Hoopfest. The mayor must have had a few choice words with Rhodes, surmised Rex.

At the bottom of the back page, a short article noted that Phil Anders, gubernatorial candidate, would be meeting with the area garden clubs and the local chapter of the Teamsters' Union. So Anders is in town, thought Rex. The rally with the Teamsters, not to mention the garden clubs, surprised him. That was Mayor Prosciutto's turf. Rex wasn't surprised to see the story buried in the paper. After all, the publisher of the *Spokane Lede* endorsed hometown Sammy Prosciutto.

Rex drained the last few heavenly drops of his Vatican and finally turned his attention to the mail. He slipped the rubber band from the bundle and looked at the package first. The return address was Shirley Pryor's. Arthur Rugula's neighbor! He quickly opened it and a dozen seed packets fell out.

First, Rugula had called him at home and now the reporter's neighbor sent a bunch of seeds to Rex's P.O. box. What was going on? Was this a joke?

Rex picked up the seed packets to examine them — tomatoes, basil, fennel, marigolds — nothing unusual. Was it some sort of code? But wait, the seed packet for the garden rocket felt lumpier than it should for such small seeds. It was inconspicuously taped shut. He carefully slit the tape with the butterknife from his croissant plate. Inside the seed packet, among the tiny rocket seeds, he found a USB stick. Maybe he and Ivy didn't need Rugula's whole computer!

He scooped up his newspaper, the mail, the package and its contents. After leaving a hefty tip for Gina, Rex rushed for the door.

Chapter 9

IVY'S BEAU

Monday Morning

While her partner started his Monday morning with coffee at Cafe Noir, Ivy led an intense self-defense course for Sophie Begonia and her female colleagues from the District Attorney's office. They practiced in the studio where Ivy had studied and earned her black belts in Judo and Aikido.

Today's lesson was the foot sweep. "The keys to making it work," Ivy instructed the class, "are constant movement, proper body position and a sense of timing."

In slow motion, she demonstrated on Sophie, who while short, still towered over Ivy by four inches. Ivy's left leg circled out from her hip and the sole of her foot stopped just as it touched Sophie's lower leg below the knee.

"Use the power from your hip and don't neglect your upper body. Your arms need to counterbalance your opponent," she added with her arms up and in front of her in a blocking position. "…this technique can be your secret weapon to knock down a much larger attacker without using excessive force. Now, let's everybody partner up and practice."

As they finished cleaning up and dressing in the locker room after class, Sophie thanked her friend. "I'm so glad you agreed to teach this self-defense class, Ivy. More women need to learn these skills. I wish the domestic violence victims I represent knew how to defend themselves."

"I'm happy to help if you organize the class," Ivy responded. "I love teaching. This is how I met Beau."

"What do you mean 'how you met Beau'? I can't believe I don't already know how you two met!" Sophie exclaimed as she fit two small, gold hoop earrings in her ears and straightened her navy suit jacket while looking in the mirror.

"You always look so professional," commented Ivy while trying to tame her own mass of fiery-red hair back into a ponytail before continuing, "I met Beau while helping teach a martial arts class for the Department of Fish and Wildlife a couple of years ago. One of his co-workers threw a fit after I flung the guy to the ground during a demonstration. Apparently, some large, machismo guys get embarrassed when tossed by tiny women. After the class, Beau came up to me and apologized for his friend's behavior. The next thing I knew, we were dating."

"Where did you go for your first date?"

"He took me to the Big Horn Outdoor Adventure Show. If you like fishing, hunting, boating and backpacking, it's the place to be and be spotted," Ivy responded. "Then we went for coffee."

"That doesn't sound like you," said Sophie. "Aren't you more of a plant person?"

"Yes, well after that, I took Beau to the Garden Expo and a tea house! I know it seems like we're different, but he's the first guy that I've dated that wasn't intimidated by my martial arts skills. And now, I'm a homicide detective, too. What guy likes to discuss cause of death during a romantic dinner?"

"Oh, I don't know. Maybe one that camps in bear country and chases poachers," laughed Sophie. "If you could see the way he looks at you, you wouldn't worry about losing out to his career or a bunch of buddies playing basketball." She hugged Ivy good-bye and added, "Say 'hi' to my big brother for me when you get to work."

Chapter 10

CARVILLE A.K.A. HOOZER

Monday Morning

After arriving at police headquarters, Rex hurried to Ivy's desk where she sat surrounded by a veritable plant jungle. Plants hung from the shelves above and beside her. They occupied major real estate on her crowded desk. They even peeked over the edge of the desk from where they stood in pots on the floor. Ivy's affinity for plants had captivated him from their first meeting.

Now, the senior detective pulled the USB stick out of the package and handed it to his tech-savvy partner. "We may not need Rugula's computer. This thumb drive was in a package his neighbor sent to me. I'm guessing Rugula suspected someone was after him and secretly sent us his files with his neighbor's help."

"It'll have to wait, Boss. The chief wants to see us right away," Ivy declared. They left the USB drive and package on her desk and headed for the chief's office.

"Good Morning. You might want to take a seat," said Chief Barney Blueblood, giving them a minute before adding, "Publicly, you two are taking the lead on investigating Jake Carville's death."

So the chief didn't think the death was an accident either, thought Rex. But what did he mean by *publicly*? The chief's face appeared indecipherable but Rex could tell he was troubled. A pile of crumpled papers surrounded the garbage can in the corner. The chief had an excellent hook shot; he didn't normally miss.

"Carville being the mayor's campaign manager, even if temporarily, makes this a high profile and a politically sensitive case. The mayor is beside himself," said Blueblood. "But that's not all. Carville wasn't really Carville. He was an undercover FBI agent."

"What?!" exclaimed Ivy, while Rex remained silent.

"His name was Henry Hoozer. He's Hoopfest Director Hal Hoozer's brother. He was investigating a national operation with ties to some big agri-chemical company in the Midwest. He wasn't supposed to be in a high profile position. I had recommended him to the mayor but only as a low level campaign staffer. It gave him cover and access to a lot of people while he worked on his case. It wasn't until the first campaign manager died and the mayor immediately promoted Hoozer that the spotlight was on him."

"That's why he looked familiar," Rex muttered aloud. "Hoopfest Director Hoozer's brother. Same lanky build, facial features and dark hair."

"This means the FBI will send someone to Spokane to take the lead on Hoozer's death behind the scenes. The Feds want to remain covert until they wrap up the investigation Hoozer was working on," explained the chief. "You'll be the public face of the investigation while cooperating with the FBI."

"So are we assuming the wreck was intentional and Hoozer was the target?" Ivy asked. "What about Jane Moregone? Maybe someone wanted to kill *her*."

"Fair point, Ivy. Murder is an equal opportunity endeavor," responded the chief. "We'll let the FBI take the lead on how their national investigation may play into the deaths. You and Rex need to explore *all* the angles and work closely with the FBI. This case is high priority. That means plant deaths and a missing garden reporter will have to wait."

Rex wasn't so sure campaign managers prevailed over plants, but the chief insisted... "I know you're not a big fan of interagency work Rex, but a couple of federal agents will be showing up here early this afternoon," continued Chief Blueblood. "I'd like you both to be here to meet them."

It was true. Rex much preferred to work alone. At least he did until Ivy joined the police force. The chief had assigned Ivy to be his partner and mentee. At times she could be too chatty for Rex, but mostly he enjoyed her perky company. She proved to be smart and capable as a detective. Her demeanor helped people open up to talking and sharing information. She had grown up with technology and brought tech skills to the job. More impressively though, she had black belts in Judo and Aikido!

Rex hoped the FBI would send Special Agent Ursula Maidger. They cooperated last year on an international bear smuggling case and Rex respected her no-nonsense manner. Rex knew they could work well together. However, even with the FBI's involvement, Rex planned to investigate all the angles. He didn't get to be Spokane's leading homicide detective by leaving any part of a case unearthed.

"We need to gather all the information we can find on Hoozer and Moregone," said Rex as he and Ivy conferred in the break room after leaving the chief's office. Every successful investigation began with a strong cappuccino according to the senior detective, who made his own. Ivy heated water for tea. "We'll also need the medical examiner's report on Hoozer and Moregone, any witness statements and the report from the forensic team that searched the crash site."

"I'll check phone records to see where Hoozer and Moregone were in the hours leading up to the crash. Should I pull the reports from the death of the first campaign manager, too?" asked Ivy.

"Those too. It's highly suspicious that two of the mayor's campaign managers died in car crashes a few days apart. I'll dig into the mayor's political rivals, Phil Anders and Tammy Hall," offered Rex. He wondered about the persistent rumors of Mayor Prosciutto's mafia ties. Maybe the FBI would have the scoop on those.

Chapter 11

SHEDDING LIGHT ON THE SCENE

Monday Afternoon

That afternoon, sunlight bathed the dog walkers and joggers exercising along the bluff next to High Drive. Blue bachelor buttons and purple vetch colored the hillside below the paved trail that lined the top of the bluff. Birds sang and flitted between the ponderosa pines. The idyllic scene belied the carnage of the night before. Police tape cordoned off the area around the crash site, dissecting the otherwise picturesque location.

After brief introductions at police headquarters, the Spokane detectives and the two FBI agents had driven to the site to view it in the daylight. It was the area beyond the police tape that attracted their attention. FBI Special Agents Hugh Bristol and Ed Dyson were from Missouri. Rex guessed them to be flatlanders from the way they walked nervously near the edge of the bluff overlooking the crash site.

"Shouldn't we be roped up or something?" asked Dyson.

"It's not as steep as it looks," replied Ivy. "Besides, there's plenty of pine trees and brush along the slope to grab, if you do take a tumble."

She blithely led the way over the edge to where the plants were matted down from the weight of the car that had slid down the hill. They carefully picked their way to a spot where the blackened vegetation indicated the vehicle came to rest and partially burned before the firefighters extinguished the flames. Black char darkened the base of a ponderosa pine that had stopped the car's slide. Ivy, who had a heart for plants, gave the trunk a sympathetic pat.

The forensics team had done a thorough job of combing the area for car parts, body parts or anything else from the crash before having the wrecked vehicle hauled out and sent to an impound facility for closer examination. The team also had taken numerous photos and measurements from the scene. Still, the detectives and the agents benefited from getting their overall impression of the crash site in person.

"I'm surprised there isn't a continuous guardrail along the whole edge," commented Agent Dyson, scanning the entire scene. Sections of guardrails lined the sharpest curves in the road, but not all of them. "This is June. How many cars slide off this bluff when the roads are icy in winter?"

"Only the ones driving too fast," responded Rex. "We have a lot of hills with curvy roads in the Northwest and guardrails are expensive. Many roads don't have rails." Then he added, "Actually, potholes cause more accidents."

"Hoozer was no dummy. If someone fooled with the vehicle, he would have noticed something wrong with the car," Agent Bristol surmised. "And I don't think he would have driven fast enough to miss a curve."

"Could he have drunk too much at the fundraiser?" asked Rex. "A DUI was the official cause of death for the mayor's last campaign manager."

"Another campaign manager died in a car wreck?" Dyson asked, incredulously.

"Earlier this month. That's when Hoozer got promoted to campaign manager," said Ivy.

"Wow, your mayor must be tough to work for," observed Dyson.

"There's another possibility. Someone forced the car off the road," said Rex, considering other options.

They returned to the top of the bluff where Rex pulled out a camera and shot a few photos to add to those taken by the forensics team. He wanted to get a larger picture of the site. He scrutinized the road in relation to the bluff. The car had caught the end of a guardrail before going over the edge. If someone ran Hoozer and Moregone off the road, they knew what they were doing. The car had launched over the edge just past a section of guardrail.

Bristol and Dyson drove to the medical examiner's office to collect Hoozer's effects while Rex and Ivy returned to police headquarters. There, a temporary office was being set up for the FBI agents in the break room.

"You know this means they're in charge of supplying doughnuts," joked Sergeant O'Dendron as he and the two detectives watched phones, computer docking stations, extension cords, a printer and more hauled into the room for Bristol and Dyson.

"And keeping the coffee pot full," added Chief Blueblood, who had come down the hall. "Here's the vehicle report and the witness statement," he said, handing a folder to Ivy, who stood closest to him.

Chapter 12

WHO'S HOOZER?

Tuesday

The next morning, Rex found Chief Blueblood in the break room filling the coffee pot. The dispatcher Darcy rushed around gathering the extra large soda cups and fast food burger wrappers scattered across the table. Half-empty coffee cups sat on dark-stained papers. Apparently, the two FBI agents had worked late last night. Rex looked disgusted. Maybe they had cleaning service at the FBI office but there wasn't one here at the Spokane PD where the chief made the most of a lean budget.

"Bristol said they'd be in later this morning," the chief scoffed with a frown. "This isn't quite what I expected. I thought the FBI would be on the ball."

It wasn't what Rex expected either. During the last case he corroborated on with the FBI, he found Special Agent Ursula Maidger highly organized and professional. Until he had worked with Maidger, his experience with the FBI was that they took local law enforcement for granted. It seemed Bristol and Dyson might reinforce that perception. Rex had arrived at the office this morning expecting to sit down with the FBI agents and strategize how to approach the case and how to divide up the investigation and responsibilities.

"We have plenty of research we can do until they arrive, Chief. What's happening with the Hoozer family? Hal Hoozer must know the guy killed in the wreck wasn't Jake Carville. What about any other family? Wife? Kids?"

"Hal's agreed not to say anything for awhile," Blueblood answered. "We're hoping the FBI will wrap this case ASAP. Apparently, Henry was getting close to completing his investigation. The only other family are the elderly parents and a sister back in Indiana. The FBI is handling family notifications."

"So how did you know Henry Hoozer, Chief?" Ivy asked.

"Years ago, I was invited to Quantico for special training. Henry was in my class. He was just a greenhorn from a farm in Indiana. We both grew up in rural areas and liked basketball. So after sitting inside all day during law enforcement training, we played lots of pickup games. We hit it off and have followed each others' careers since then.

"His brother Hal, of course, was a basketball standout for Indiana State University before joining the Gonzaga Bulldogs as an assistant coach. That was before Hoopfest hired him as the director a few years ago.

"This past spring, Henry contacted me to say he would be working on an investigation in our area and needed a cover. I hooked him up with the mayor's campaign. He was supposed to be in a low profile position — not a campaign manager for a gubernatorial race. Like most people, he probably had trouble saying 'no' to the mayor." The chief looked glum.

"Wow! Henry's death couldn't come at a worse time for Hal. So soon before Hoopfest," said Ivy. "Were they close?"

"Yeah, this must be hard on Hal," Blueblood admitted. "Hal suffered a double hit, you know. He's friends with PJ Moregone, who lost his wife in the accident, too."

Rex made a mental note to ask Molly Murrow what she knew about Jane Moregone and Jake Carville. If there was more than a professional relationship, Molly would know. She knew the dirt on everyone in town. He hoped she was still speaking with him. He still hadn't heard back from her regarding his lunch invitation.

"Sorry for the loss of your friend," Rex said, remembering that Chief Blueblood and Henry Hoozer had been colleagues.

"Thanks, Rex. I'm confident you'll find out who killed Henry and we'll bring them to justice."

By now, Rex had filled his own cup with a cappuccino and Ivy had her tea. They returned to their separate desks to do their homework as the senior detective fondly called it. A voice message on his phone relayed that Molly agreed to meet for lunch. The day looked better already.

After getting the names of Moregone's and Hoozer's phone carriers, Ivy began obtaining phone records. Rex searched online for Henry Hoozer but couldn't find much information beyond newspaper clippings of high school and college basketball games confirming Hoozer's athletic talent. It didn't surprise Rex. After all, Hoozer was an undercover agent.

The digital background search on PJ Moregone revealed a different story. A *Spokane Biz Zine* feature caught Rex's attention. The one-year old article highlighted Moregone's extensive career in the community. It credited his financial savvy with helping many local businesses, including Hoopfest, grow. One short paragraph referenced a freelance job with a Wes Larch development project — the 10,000 square foot basketball court in Riverfront Park. Rex considered whether the job involved a conflict of interest. Had Hoozer been investigating underhanded dealings between the city, Larch and Moregone?

When the two FBI agents still had not appeared by lunch time, Rex left to meet Molly at the Noodle Fusion Bistro. He took her a bouquet of purple hyacinth and peach-colored roses as a peace offering. He planned to eat a large piece of humble pie for lunch.

Rex and Molly didn't squabble often, but when they did, it was usually work-related. They both had a strong work ethic. And they were both stubborn! At times, the nature of her investigative reporting conflicted with his need to protect the integrity of a case. Although, Rex could also recall plenty of times that Molly's investigative skills had helped him solve a case.

If aging had weakened Rex's physical vigor, it had also made him wiser. Relationships were important. To keep them, it sometimes required making the initial apology. He definitely wanted to preserve his relationship with Molly Murrow.

He looked forward to making up with Molly and eating at his brother-in-law Nobu's restaurant. Owner and chef Nobu Hiyamugi made the best spaghetti Bolognese in town. Even better than Mama Begonia. For that, he had Rex's undying admiration.

Chapter 13

A WITNESS

Tuesday Afternoon

Ivy went home for lunch so she could feed and walk Yukon. Beau had left his dog with her while he was out of town on a case. At least Yukon was available for cuddling.

She decided to take Yukon along the High Drive bluff path. What would have taken her five minutes, took twenty as the Husky stopped to exchange sniffs with all the other dogs walking with their persons. She wondered what mysteries he might be solving. They came to the crime scene tape and stopped. Ivy peered down the slope toward the scarred ponderosa.

"Excuse me," came a timid voice from behind her. "Are you one of the police officers that was here looking at where the car went over the edge?"

Ivy turned and saw a teenage girl with large eyes, auburn hair and a matching-colored Rhodesian ridgeback straining at his leash. A smaller, tan, mixed-breed dog off-leash greeted Yukon with a friendly sniff. Ivy addressed the girl, "I'm Officer Lizei. I was here yesterday. Were you here, too? What's your name?"

"Jill. I saw the crash. And I saw you here yesterday. This is where I walk my dogs."

"You saw the crash? You were here that night? What did you see?"

"It was dark and raining so it was hard to see anything. But we did notice a big pickup truck chasing the car that crashed. It kept ramming into the car. It rammed the little car multiple times and pushed it over the edge. Then the truck sped away. It happened so quickly."

"We? You were with someone else? And where were you, exactly, when you saw the vehicles?"

43

"I was with my boyfriend. I wasn't supposed to be, so please don't let my parents know. We were in his car, just over there," Jill said, pointing to a spot a few feet away on the other side of the road. "We left when the cops came."

She led Ivy to where she and her boyfriend had been the night of the crash.

The detective took in the scene. If the pickup truck driver was focused on the car, he probably didn't see Jill and her boyfriend, especially in the dark. He probably thought it was the perfect murder, thought Ivy.

"Did you see the driver? What do you remember about the truck?" she asked.

"It was a big pickup, you know the kind that are jacked up on huge tires? I couldn't tell what brand but it looked like it was black or dark gray and it had a tool box. I couldn't see the driver. The rain made it hard to see."

"How about your boyfriend? What's his name? Can I talk with him, too?"

Jill gave Ivy her boyfriend's and her own name and phone number. "I'm sorry we didn't stay," she added. "I just didn't want to get in trouble."

"It's okay, You did the right thing by telling me," said Ivy. "You won't get in trouble with the police." She couldn't vouch for Jill's parents though.

Ivy tugged on the dog's collar. "Come on Yukon. Time to leave your new friends. We need to get back and let Rex know about the pickup truck."

Chapter 14

INTERAGENCY TANGLES

Tuesday Afternoon

By the time Ivy returned to police headquarters, FBI agents Bristol and Dyson were discussing the case with Rex in the break room.

Rex had started a list of people involved in the case. First, the victims Jake Carville (a.k.a. Henry Hoozer) and Jane Moregone. He wrote "Tip Seeborn" off to the side, not knowing yet whether the incidents were connected. He could add names as the investigation broadened.

The forensics team had determined that Jane was driving the car when it crashed. A wealthy socialite, Jane volunteered at the Humane Society, where she helped retrain rescue dogs. Rex wrote down Jane's husband PJ's name also — PJ Moregone, Accountant and Director of Moregone Capital Firm.

From Molly Murrow, Rex had learned that PJ's financial savvy didn't translate to the home front. The Moregones had recently suffered financial setbacks. Molly also shared that rumors existed about a possible dalliance between Jane Moregone and Jake Carville. Upon further investigation, Rex learned that PJ Moregone, recently, had increased the life insurance coverage on Jane.

As the FBI agents knew, Jake Carville was really Henry Hoozer. As Carville, he was single and had worked on Mayor Prosciutto's gubernatorial campaign for the past six months, mostly writing speeches and press releases and other behind the scenes work. His fictitious resume indicated that he had worked on a number of smaller campaigns in the Midwest. His real communication and organizational skills caught the attention of Mayor Sammy Prosciutto, who had quickly promoted Carville to acting campaign manager upon the death of his first campaign manager, Tip

45

Seeborn. Carville was well-liked by his colleagues and didn't have any known enemies.

"What about Prosciutto? Two campaign managers dead in less than two weeks. Maybe someone's trying to derail his campaign for governor," opined Bristol.

"Bumping off Prosciutto himself would minimize the number of murders needing to be committed," answered Rex. "But Phil Anders is the top candidate running against Prosciutto. Anders is the mayor of Tacoma, Washington's third largest city. He's made a real effort to clean up Tacoma over the past few years and is threatening to take away Prosciutto's support with the green vote. The other candidate is Lieutenant Governor Tammy Hall. She has a well-oiled political machine in Western Washington." He added their names to his list of potentially involved people.

Rex hadn't found any information on Henry Hoozer other than what he had learned from Chief Blueblood. He hoped the FBI agents could fill in the blanks.

"Not happening," said Bristol. "We can't risk blowing open the case Hoozer was working on."

Bristol reminded Rex why the Spokane detective didn't care for interagency work. Whether due to a lack of trust, fragile egos or protecting one's turf, some individuals just didn't play well with others. Apparently they forgot what they learned in kindergarten.

"Or we could work collaboratively and crack Hoozer's murder case a lot quicker," Rex offered, curtly.

"What else did the forensics report reveal?" asked Bristol, ignoring Spokane's top homicide detective.

Ivy pulled out the report. "Unfortunately, the fire and the car's tumble down the hill may have obscured some evidence. But the forensic technicians did find small amounts of black paint corresponding with dents on the rear, passenger side of the car. The black paint came from another vehicle.

"The evidence suggests the possibility that another vehicle ran Carville/Hoozer and Moregone off the road. This theory was confirmed by a young woman I met while walking along the bluff during lunch. She and her boyfriend witnessed a large, dark-colored pickup truck chasing the car and running it off the road. I have the young woman's statement but haven't talked with her boyfriend yet."

Ivy continued. "I made some calls and discovered that Carville/Hoozer and Moregone were at a campaign fundraising event for Mayor Prosciutto at June Bloomenthal's home for about three hours prior to the crash. They left the house 15 minutes before the 9-1-1 call came in about the car going off the road."

"Good work, Lizei. See if anyone at the event left about the same time and may have seen the black pickup," said Bristol. "Maybe one of the attendees at the event saw the truck and got a look at the driver. Or maybe one of the attendees drove the pickup."

Ivy glanced over at Rex with a—"who put this guy in charge?"— look.

"We did get back the medical examiner's report," offered Dyson. "Both Hoozer and Moregone died from injuries sustained in the crash. Neither of them had alcohol or drugs in their systems."

"If the deaths of the two campaign managers are related, the perpetrator decided to be more direct this time," observed Rex, feeling a bit pushed to the side by the FBI agents.

"I'd like you two to follow up with Jake Carville's campaign connections and with this PJ Moregone fellow," said Bristol. "We'll pay a visit to Hal Hoozer and the leads from Henry's investigation. Let's meet back here tomorrow afternoon. I'd like to see what you find."

As he and Ivy left the break room, Rex pondered how he could search for Arthur Rugula while following up on insurance claims and questioning political candidates.

"Hey Rex, why so sullen?" asked Sergeant O'Dendren as he encountered his colleagues heading down the hall.

"Let's just say I don't like games," answered Rex.

"Speaking of games, we're throwing a Hoopfest party at the O'Dendren estate on Friday. We're barbecuing a bunch of dogs and burgers; shooting some hoops. You're both invited. You can bring that hot boyfriend of yours, Ivy."

Rex thought he heard Ivy mutter, "I wish."

Chapter 15

CONNECTIONS

Wednesday Morning

Rex needed a strong espresso to steel himself for the day ahead. He wasn't looking forward to interacting with Bristol and Dyson. Plus, he and Chief Blueblood were scheduled to discuss the case with Mayor Prosciutto. With the FBI agents commandeering the break room, Rex chose to stop at Cafe Noir to fortify himself for the day before meeting the chief at the mayor's office.

Chief Blueblood had secured the FBI's blessing to share Henry Hoozer's true identity with the mayor. Did this mean Bristol and Dyson didn't think the mayor had any mafia connections? Maybe they hoped that the mayor might let slip some incriminating information?

After entering City Hall, Rex and the chief waited in the anteroom outside the mayor's office while Mayor Prosciutto finished meeting with other visitors. At least the receptionist offered them espresso while they waited. The perks of having a mayor with Italian heritage, mused Rex.

He was surprised to see the odd pairing of Wes Larch and Judge Rudy Marconi leaving the mayor's office as he and the chief were ushered in. During the subsequent conversation between Chief Blueblood and the mayor, Rex learned that Larch and Marconi were helping Prosciutto rebuild his campaign staff.

"They're finding me a new campaign manager. How am I supposed to run a campaign with campaign managers driving over cliffs every week? And now you're telling me Carville wasn't even a real campaign manager?" Sammy Prosciutto fumed. The exasperated mayor paced back and forth behind his large, opulent desk.

Rex couldn't help but notice the similarity between the mayor and the man at the center of a black and white photo prominently displayed on the wall. The sharply dressed man in the photo stood on a stage before a massive crowd in Sicily. Behind him, sat two shifty looking characters. The man was Sammy Prosciutto's great-grandfather who had immigrated to the United States during the early twentieth century. Infamously, he ran a bootleg business in Spokane during the prohibition era before being killed by gangsters. Then, Sammy's grandfather took over the family business.

Turning away from the photo and looking in the opposite direction, Rex could see out a large window with a view of Riverfront Park. Set-up for Hoopfest had started. Mayor Prosciutto would soon speak to a crowd there. Statewide media would cover the event. The mayor's political rivals could only hope for such a high-profile venue.

"Judge Marconi and Wes Larch will find an excellent replacement," offered Chief Blueblood. He was too diplomatic to remind the mayor that Carville hadn't intended to be a campaign manager.

"The FBI requested we keep Carville's real identity secret until they've closed out the case he was working on so as not to compromise the investigation," said the chief.

"Compromise the case?! They better hope they don't compromise my campaign! What are they working on anyway? Is it something that could make Spokane look bad? Or make me look bad? I've busted my butt to make Spokane a place we can be proud of.

"Just look," he said, waving toward Riverfront Park. "We'll be hosting the world's largest three-on-three basketball tournament in a matter of days. Thousands of people come from all over the nation to play and to watch. What other city can boast of events like Hoopfest? Or Bloomsday? We've put Spokane on the map!"

Rex thought maybe the Gonzaga basketball teams had put Spokane on the map. But he did concur with the mayor. The Lilac City outmatched larger cities when it came to hosting major events. And Riverfront Park with the Spokane River winding through the middle of downtown was just one of many lovely parks and natural areas beautifying the city.

After placating the mayor and assuring his cooperation, Chief Blueblood and Rex called on Hoopfest Director Hal Hoozer. Hoozer's office was located on the first floor of a tall building about half a mile from City Hall. The plate glass windows looked out onto Riverside Avenue, one of the many streets that would soon be thronged with basketball players and fans. Nerf balls and real basketballs covered Hoozer's office floor and a hoop hung above the door. Now that's work-life balance, thought Rex.

"Hi, Chief. Welcome," said Hoozer, extending his large hand when Blueblood and Begonia entered his office.

"Hi, Hal. You probably already know Detective Rex Begonia," introduced the chief. "He's our number one homicide detective in Spokane. We're all really sorry about your brother. FBI agents Bristol and Dyson told you what happened?"

"Yeah. They were here earlier and asked me to keep quiet about Henry posing as Carville. They said they were finishing up his case and weren't sure if it had anything to do with Henry's death, or if somebody had it in for Carville. They said your officers would be working the Carville angle.

"I told them I wouldn't say anything, at least until Hoopfest is over. But we can't hide this thing forever. Our family will want to recognize Henry's death."

"We'll do everything we can to find Henry's murderer," Chief Blueblood assured his friend.

"Thanks, Barney," Hoozer continued. "This news will be tough on Mom and Dad. Mom always worried about Henry working in law enforcement. He could have made a killing in the NBA but he wanted a career that helped people. He loved being a cop — despite the risks."

"Did Henry say anything to you about the case he was working on?" Rex asked.

"No, I knew he was an undercover agent and he was looking into something tied to an investigation back in the Midwest. That's about the extent of what I knew. We talked basketball, not work. Or not his work, anyway," said Hoozer. "I told the FBI agents the same thing. They just left here before you arrived. I gave them a key I had to Henry's apartment."

"Thanks," said Rex. It seemed he'd have to find a way to get Bristol to share information about Henry's investigation.

"I forgot to tell those FBI agents that there was a newspaper reporter with an unusual name asking around for Henry," said Hal. "I didn't think much about it at first, but he didn't ask for Carville; he specifically requested Henry Hoozer. That's what was so strange. He left without leaving any contact information."

Rugula! It had to be, thought Rex. "Was the reporter's name Arthur Rugula, by chance?" he asked. "When did you see him?"

"Yeah, that sounds about right. He was here a little over a week ago. A few days before Henry died," Hal replied.

"One more thing. I know there's rumors about Henry having an affair with Jane Moregone. Don't believe it. It's not true. Jane's death has been devastating enough for PJ without the vicious rumors. And the timing couldn't be worse. Aside from tax season, this is the busiest time of the year for him."

"Is PJ in the office today? Any chance we can talk with him?" Rex asked.

"He's out at the moment. He's taking care of things and making arrangements for Jane's funeral. He won't be out long. This is a busy time of the year, even for our contractors."

"Do you have his home phone number?" Rex tried another approach.

After departing from Hal Hoozer's office with Moregone's number, the chief and Rex stopped for lunch at the Fusion Noodle Bistro. The detective felt a twinge of guilt. Until the recent visit with Hal Hoozer, the dramatic deaths of Carville/Henry Hoozer and Jane Moregone pushed Rugula's disappearance aside. Hopefully, the garden reporter didn't suffer a similar fate.

For once, Rex barely paid attention to his pasta. He twirled the noodles absentmindedly on his fork and wondered what they would find on Arthur Rugula's thumb drive.

Chapter 16

A MESSAGE FROM RUGULA

Wednesday Afternoon

"Hi, Boss," Ivy piped up from her desk behind a fortress of plants when Rex finally arrived at police headquarters that afternoon.

"I know the chief told us the Moregone/Carville case is our highest priority, but wait until you see this," she said, not even waiting for an acknowledgement and holding up a thumb drive. She slid the stick into the side of the USB port on the computer.

"It's the one Arthur Rugula sent. I opened it during lunch break and took a look. Not like I've had any exciting lunch dates or anything lately."

"Serendipitous," said Rex.

"What's that, Boss?"

"I was just thinking about Rugula's thumb drive during lunch."

"Oh," said Ivy. "Anyway, the stick has a bunch of folders you might find interesting."

After a security scan of the USB stick, four electronic file folders popped up on Ivy's computer screen. The first one was labeled Articles. Other folders included Contacts, Research and Site Visits. Ivy clicked open Articles. It contained a news story about the mysterious plant mortalities in Manito Park gardens. Additional articles focused on the puzzling plant problem throughout the county.

"Did you hear about this mysterious plant disease in the county?" Ivy asked. "Pops told me it's some kind of poisoning. People have been losing thousands of dollars worth of plants." Ivy's father, Joe Lizei owned and operated Lizei Nursery, famous in the Northwest for its quality plants. "He's worried about losing business if a solution isn't found soon. People often blame nurseries when their plants die."

Rex remembered Molly reporting on the demise of plants in Manito. He'd have to ask her if she collaborated with Rugula when putting together the story. Maybe she knew how to get in touch with the reporter.

Ivy opened the Contact folder next. She and Rex recognized the names of the leaders of many of Spokane's garden clubs, select local farmers and others in the gardening, landscape or farming communities. A PhD next to some of the names indicated possible professors or research scientists.

"Do you see a name on this list that stands out?" she asked Rex.

"Yes, I do indeed. Jake Carville."

Rex doubted the frugal Rugula would be a big political donor. Could the connection be that Carville, a.k.a. Henry Hoozer, and Arthur Rugula were investigating the same mystery of the plant deaths? Did the garden reporter somehow stumble on Hoozer seeking the same information? Could Rugula hold the secret to solving Hoozer/ Carville's death? Was he even still alive?

The Research folder contained scientific studies and news articles about various pesticides and plant diseases. "This might come in handy later, but there's so much here it's hard to know what exactly Rugula was working on," Ivy acknowledged. "Maybe the Site Visit folder will be more helpful."

Files in the Site Visit folder supported articles Rugula had written, including appointments with Head Gardener Toni Fritts at Manito Park, farmer Nate Nettle at Near Nature Farm and Community Garden Supervisor Angela Marconi at the Airway Heights Corrections Center. Rugula had also made a visit to SoilCycle Inc., a compost company. Interestingly, Sal Prosciutto, the mayor's brother owned SoilCycle, Inc.

"Without Rugula here to tell us what this all means, we'll have to follow in his footsteps and hope they lead us to him, and possibly Hoozer's and Moregone's murderer," said Rex. "Let's plan for a field day tomorrow."

"What about the FBI?" asked Ivy. "Didn't Bristol want us to follow up with Carville's political connections and the Jane Moregone angle while they investigated Hoozer's case?"

"Already on it. Phil Anders is speaking to the Teamsters' Union tonight. I plan to be there. Nothing says we can't work multiple cases at once," announced Rex. "We'll just search for the missing Rugula while following up on our part of the murder investigation."

Chapter 17

BROTHERHOOD

Wednesday Evening

Rex pulled into the parking lot at the Teamsters' Hall fifteen minutes before the start of the rally that evening. A small group of men and a few women stood outside the open door, taking final drags on their cigarettes before going inside to sit for an hour. The "International Brotherhood of Teamsters" sign above the door gave Rex an idea.

His police union brothers and sisters in Tacoma could give him the lowdown on Phil Anders the candidate. Who knew a big city mayor better than those serving in police headquarters? Rex pulled out his phone and called his buddy, the senior detective on Tacoma's major crimes unit. "Hi Pierce, you gotta minute?"

Ten minutes later the Spokane detective decided it was time to get a sense of the public-facing candidate Anders. He exited his car and stepped into the union hall.

"Meet the next Governor of Washington State — Phil Anders," shouted the evening's moderator as Rex slipped into the back of the room where he could easily survey the scene and get a good view of the featured speaker. A boisterous crowd filled the rows of folding chairs in front of the stage. Electric fans whirred on either side of the room as they circulated air in an attempt to cool the packed room. It was still sweltering.

Anders stepped to the podium. He looked like he walked off the cover of a GQ magazine. In his early 50s, Anders had the figure of a man who worked out every day. He wore his full head of dark hair tousled and his necktie loosened over a crisp white shirt with rolled sleeves. He had ditched the jacket that matched the dress pants. Despite his attempts at looking casual, he faced a crowd that already considered him an outsider.

55

Most of the audience members wore T-shirts with shorts or jeans. Many sported ball caps, some with sunglasses, despite being indoors. They fidgeted in the heat and demanded to know why they should support Anders for Governor. After all, Mayor Sammy Prosciutto could bring an Eastern Washington perspective to the Governor's mansion.

Anders slyly agreed they raised a good point. "You need to know that I bleed crimson and gray, however. I did my undergraduate work at Washington State University, just a few miles south of here." Having established his Eastern Washington credentials, he transitioned to a topic more dear to this crowd. "More importantly, I'll get you that north-south freeway," he promised. "I have the political savvy and the connections to make it happen. Your current mayor didn't get the job done and he won't as Governor."

"Boo!" yelled someone in the back of the room.

"Shut up! Give the guy a chance," shouted another attendee at the heckler.

Rex had heard that pledge before. For decades, politicians promised a north-south freeway. During Mayor Prosciutto's term, the first section was built but completion remained distant. Maybe Anders' connections were more powerful?

Anders droned on about his work with the unions in Tacoma and how important transportation and the movement of goods through the Seattle and Tacoma ports benefited the Teamsters and their families, even here in Eastern Washington.

As the mayor of Washington's third largest city, Phil Anders rivaled Sammy Prosciutto in more ways than as competing gubernatorial candidates. Both men led cities that vied for recognition in the shadow of the state's largest city, Seattle. Spokane claimed the number two spot with just a few thousand more people living within its city limits than the 220,000 inhabiting Tacoma.

Both candidates took pride in having beautified their cities while boosting their economies. Mayor Prosciutto focused on parks and the environment, while Mayor Anders concentrated on the visual arts. Rex's call to his buddy Pierce revealed that Phil Anders had an eye for beauty that went beyond the arts.

Allegedly, Anders was engaged to Miss Washington years ago while in graduate school. The engagement fell through and Anders married the daughter of a Seattle billionaire instead. An affair with the now former Miss Washington followed two years later. High-powered friends helped Anders cover up the transgression. Anders paid off the young woman to avoid a scandal early in his political career. Most intriguing about the story — the young woman, Eve Pomme, went on to marry Sammy Prosciutto, Spokane Mayor.

Did Mayor Prosciutto know about his wife's romantic past? wondered Rex. Were the two mayors more than political rivals? Rex hoped to question Anders who had just finished his speech. By the time the detective wove through the crowd to get to the front of the room, Anders' political aides had whisked the candidate out a side door. They were nowhere to be seen.

Chapter 18

In Rugula's Footsteps

Thursday

"By all pitching in, we will make this place look spectacular before visitors descend upon the city this weekend. They may be in town for basketball, but most people visit Manito Park while they're here," said Head Gardener Toni Fritts, who was addressing a sizable crowd before her when Rex and Ivy arrived at Manito Park's Duncan Garden.

A sweet scent of blossoms filled the cool, morning air, but the forecast called for rising temperatures — into the high 90s. In gloved hands, the park's staff each held a plant map of the garden beds where they had laboriously replaced contaminated soil during the past week. "Let's plant!" yelled Fritts.

Spokane's garden club leaders had pulled together a team of volunteers, who now picked up containers of flowers and spread out among the beds to transplant the annuals. Like a swarm of bees, they busily buzzed around the beds, quickly replacing the dead flowers that had been removed by park staff.

"So glad you could join us, detectives," Toni Fritts said when she spotted Rex and Ivy. "Are you here to help replant Duncan Garden?"

"Actually, we came to ask you about why the garden had to be replanted," responded Rex. "We did see the news story about the plant die-off. Did you ever discover what caused it?"

"Poison," answered Toni. "Soil samples that we sent to the WSU labs came back positive for Defender. It's a synthetic herbicide that kills broadleaved weeds in lawns. The problem is it also kills broadleaf flowers, like the ones we had in Duncan Garden.

"People used to spread Defender on their lawns until the state banned it for residential use years ago. Until the ban, the city collected the treated lawn clippings as part of the yard waste pickup. The waste was composted and later sold commercially," she continued.

"Evidently, the herbicide doesn't break down in the composting process. So, it can still kill plants when the compost is added to the soil. We're not sure how it ended up here recently, though," Fritts said.

"And that's the story Arthur Rugula was digging into?" Ivy asked.

"Yes, he met with me and the park staff three weeks ago. The garden club leaders joined us. We had quite the discussion. The Defender problem was widespread in the county. It not only affected parks but many garden club members reported losing plants too. I told Arthur about sending the soil samples to WSU."

"Did Rugula follow-up with you after the meeting?" Rex asked.

"Now that you mention it, no he didn't. I thought for sure he would be here today to take pictures and report on the replanting."

It was easy to overlook Rugula, thought Rex. The unassuming garden reporter had thick glasses, thinning hair and a diminutive stature. He tended to quietly blend in to his surroundings unless agitated, then he could be quite peppery.

"Come back to see the garden and be sure to stop by for Art in the Park this weekend. "We'll be setting up for that too," said Fritts, after the detectives concluded their questioning. "We will be featuring watercolor paintings by local artist Megan Perkins."

"Perkins? That sounds like an artist I would like," said Rex, thinking it might be time for a coffee break.

They said their good-byes to Toni Fritts, who asked Ivy to thank her father for the plant donation from Lizei Nursery. Then, they headed toward the police vehicle where Ivy climbed in behind the wheel.

"Next stop, Near Nature Farm," announced Rex as he buckled up.

Chapter 19

RUGULA'S THEORIES

Thursday

"Near disaster is what it is," Nate Nettle grumbled to Rex and Ivy over cups of chicory coffee and herbal tea after they settled in at his ten-acre vegetable farm on the south end of Spokane.

"Thanks to PEA-S we defeated Wes Larch and saved our farmland from development, but now we're dealing with this new issue. We lost many of our crops: tomatoes, peppers, peas, beans and potatoes. The leaves got all deformed and curled up. It was almost a total loss. We sent samples to the WSU lab.

"The toxicology reports that came back showed high levels of the herbicide Defender in the plants and the soil. But we didn't use Defender anywhere on our farm! That's why Rugula was here. He heard other farmers and gardeners were having similar problems. He was trying to find out how Defender got into all the gardens when no one had actually used it. We brought together the farm members of PEA-S to meet with Rugula here on the farm."

Defender, again. Rex recalled when Spokane made national news decades ago due to Defender being discovered in the city compost. The active chemical in the herbicide remained potent even after plants sprayed with it were composted. Since then, the state banned the chemical from use on lawns, except for golf courses. Ivy was probably too young to remember the incident. If Defender was showing up in the Spokane area again, the People for Environmental Agriculture—Spokane (PEA-S) would be dialed in, for sure.

"Did Rugula share any theories he had?" asked Rex.

60

"Well, he did ask about our composting. Mostly, we use the compost we make on farm but this year we had to bring in additional compost. We hauled it in from Airway Heights Corrections Center. They produce more waste material than they can use composting for their little community garden."

"Did Rugula mention if he was working with anyone else in his investigation?" Ivy asked.

"He talked about a researcher, a Dr. Ájrah, doing the lab work at WSU. He also hinted at working with someone on a national investigation, but he didn't give any names. I hope Rugula finds out who's responsible," replied Nate.

"We have to add massive amounts of clean soil to the vegetable beds to dilute the Defender. And we won't be able to sell any produce grown in the affected beds as organic, so it's a huge financial hit. If whoever's responsible isn't held accountable or we don't get financial help, we won't be able to keep farming."

Rex thought about how Papa Begonia's produce business relied on these local farmers and he shared Nate's desire for justice. He was determined to solve this compost investigation and find out who and what was rotten.

"We'll see what we can dig up at the Airway Heights Corrections Center's community garden next," declared Rex to Ivy. "It was also on Rugula's list of visits. With any luck, we'll get to the root of this problem soon."

After saying their good-byes to Nate, the two detectives headed to the corrections center on the plains west of Spokane. It had been three years since either of them had seen Angela Marconi, incarcerated for her role in the Murder at Manito case. Given her past garden club leadership, it was no surprise that she was now the inmate who organized and oversaw the community garden at the facility. They weren't sure whether Angela would welcome their visit though, given their past history together.

Chapter 20

THE SOURCE

Thursday

As it turned out, Angela Marconi was in a good mood that afternoon. She had received word that morning that she was eligible for early release in six months due to exemplary behavior. Still, they had to conduct their meeting in the secure visiting room after passing the security screening.

Despite the orange jumpsuit attire, Angela Marconi still resembled Sophia Loren with her shiny dark hair, flawless skin, blinding smile and long lashes. Only the stains on the knees of the jumpsuit hinted that she spent hours working in a garden.

"Detectives Begonia and Lizei. It's been a long time," she said, staring them straight in the eyes and drawing out the word "long." "Whatever do I owe the pleasure of this visit to?"

Rex, who knew Angela and her family for years prior to her incarceration, couldn't bring himself to address her by anything but her first name. "Hello, Angela. I heard the good news about your early release. Your family must be happy," he said.

They all engaged in a bit of awkward small talk before Rex came to the point of the visit, "We're hoping you can help us with a new case. We learned that you started a community garden here. And that Arthur Rugula may have visited you about a plant problem in the garden. Is that true?"

"Yes, the garden's about half an acre. Ten other women and I take care of it. Thank goodness for the garden! It's what's kept me sane all this time and it's so inspiring to see women who have never gardened before realize the benefits of tending to plants. It's remarkable how invested they have become. Some of the long-term residents have been discussing planting a perennial garden.

"But, this year, most of our plants mysteriously died. I wasn't sure what the problem was and I didn't have access to the Master Gardener Program like I did on the outside. So, I described what was happening in a letter to Julia. Did you know — she's studying Horticulture now at Washington State University? — It wasn't long after that, Arthur Rugula came out here to do a story."

"Did you find out what killed the plants?" Ivy asked.

"Arthur took samples of the plants and the soils and sent them to a professor at WSU. He was going to write another article after he learned why the plants were dying, but I haven't heard back from him."

"Did you add compost to the garden beds?" Rex inquired.

"Of course. Why? Was compost the problem?"

"It might have contained an herbicide called Defender," Ivy answered. "What's the source for your compost?"

"Did you see that sign for SoilCycle, Inc. next to the corrections center when you arrived? That's where all the yard waste and food scraps collected by the county go to be turned into compost," explained Angela. "Of course, the corrections center produces enough of our own waste material, but it's all mixed together. SoilCycle has the equipment and the corrections center supplies the cheap, inmate labor. In exchange for the labor, the corrections center gets free compost for our community garden."

"Who manages the composting operation here?" asked Rex.

"Mickey Gronk is the lead for the corrections center. Locally, he's known as Gunk. He's an employee but he really should be an inmate," Angela said disgustedly. "Gunk and a couple of other guards oversee a prison crew that's allowed off site to work in SoilCycle's composting facility. Word among the inmates is he's running a narcotics operation, bringing drugs in with the compost. I stay as far from Gunk as possible."

"Did Rugula ask about Gronk? Or the compost?" inquired Ivy.

"He did take copious notes on our growing practices and what we are growing. We probably discussed the composting, but I don't think we talked about Gunk or the connection with SoilCycle. I might have mentioned getting compost from SoilCycle." Angela's expression grew serious. "I wish I could be more helpful but I really don't know any more than that. Everything is more difficult here."

"Thanks. You've been extremely helpful," Rex reassured her. "And I'm sure your associates here are grateful for the garden you've created."

"I don't know about that. Some of these jailbirds don't like vegetables on the menu. Maybe someone had it in for our little garden. The last time the cooks served up fresh broccoli, the cafeteria erupted in a food fight."

"And I thought it was just kids that didn't like to eat their vegetables," said Ivy.

"Yes, well you might say it's a case of arrested development here," quipped Angela.

Rex quietly groaned.

Chapter 21

DIGGING INTO COMPOST

Thursday

"That completes the garden and crop visits on Rugula's list," declared Ivy, after she and Rex left the Airway Heights Correction Center. "That just leaves SoilCycle, Inc."

A loud rumbling reminded Rex that the afternoon waned.

"Sorry about that, Boss. That's my stomach. I skipped breakfast this morning." Ivy looked sheepish.

"I'm getting hungry myself. Let's make a pit stop in Airway Heights and then we'll swing back by SoilCycle to see if we can make sense of this compost muck."

A few minutes later, Ivy pulled into the Olive & Feta, a drive-thru serving Middle Eastern fare. Rex ordered a large gyro and Greek fries. Ivy chose a vegetarian gyro with hummus. The smell of warm garlic, oregano and lemon wafting from the mounds of food increased their appetites. Ivy's stomach growled loudly again.

"We might have to get the engine checked," Rex commented. "That noise is getting louder."

"Ha! This should take care of it," Ivy responded before taking a bite of her gyro. "Wonder how our FBI friends are doing?" she continued after swallowing. "They seemed a bit — I don't know — proprietary."

"Yeah, it looks like Arthur Rugula connected with Hoozer, a.k.a. Carville, over the contaminated compost situation. But I'm not sure why the FBI would be interested in plants dying in Spokane," mused Rex.

"Could it be a connection with the drugs at the correction center? Could the corrections center be tied to the new drug cartel the chief mentioned?" asked Ivy.

"Maybe, but if that were the case, I think Chief Blueblood would have our own narcotics unit working on it before calling in the FBI. Usually, drug operations get sniffed out locally and then the big dogs are brought in if it looks like the operation extends beyond the local jurisdictions.

"And, let's not forget Moregone," Rex continued. "It's still possible that the homicide is unrelated to a contaminated compost investigation and Hoozer was just collateral damage. Moregone did increase Jane's insurance coverage. We'll visit PJ Moregone this afternoon, after we stop at SoilCycle. Remember, Mayor Prosciutto's brother Sal Prosciutto owns SoilCycle."

Having taken care of the top priority, lunch, the two detectives backtracked toward SoilCycle, Inc., located next to the Airway Heights Correction Center. They pulled the car onto the property, surrounded by a razor-wire topped fence. Except for the heaps of food waste and plant material in different stages of decomposition and the large equipment turning and moving the piles, the site looked like it could be part of the corrections center.

As they exited the vehicle, Rex took a deep whiff of air. "Ahh! It never ceases to amaze me how a bunch of kitchen scraps mixed with yard waste, sprinkled with water, and mixed together can smell so earthy. You would think it would smell like rotting food."

"Well, seeing as how I feed compost to my discerning plants, I'm glad it's not stinky," said Ivy.

A squat, grimy, cement-block office building stood a few yards from the compost piles. A young man in stained brown coveralls and a SoilCycle, Inc. ball cap looked up from a desk heaped with papers when the two detectives entered. He set down a raunchy magazine and asked, "Can I help you?"

"I'm Detective Begonia and this is Detective Lizei. Is Sal Prosciutto in today?"

"Sal's the owner, but he don't really work here. He don't come round much."

"Are you the manager then?" Ivy asked.

"Nah. That'd be Kevin Greene. He ain't here either," the young man said. He looked suspiciously at the two detectives. "He's still at lunch. Can I tell him why you were here?"

"We'll come back later," said Rex, ignoring the question. "When can we find Mr. Greene at this facility?"

"He's here between eight and five most days. Sometimes he's got errands, so — hard to say. I'll tell him you was here."

"Thanks," said Rex and left a business card with a phone number where he could be reached. "Mind if we take a quick look around while we're here?"

The young man seemed hesitant. He glanced at the business card and finally replied, "Just keep close to the building. Wouldn't want anything unfortunate to happen to you. Big equipment out there, you know." He gave them a piercing stare.

After exiting the building, the two detectives quickly slipped around the corner and headed toward the backside of the office. They saw a work crew of men in coveralls about 50 yards away. One of the men poured a substance from a barrel into a 1,500-gallon water tank.

The two detectives watched in fascination. The loudness of machinery moving and grinding prevented conversation. A front-end loader dropped large chunks of woody debris into a massive tub-shaped machine that chewed up the material. Nearby, one of the inmate crew members drove a tractor pulling what looked like an upside down u-shaped frame on wheels. An auger stretched between the two sides of the frame. It turned the compost in 12-foot wide rows as the machine passed over the material. A second water tank, pulled by an off-road vehicle, sprayed water onto the 200-foot long compost piles. Rex and Ivy, both being avid gardeners, composted at home for their own gardens but this was composting on a much larger scale!

At the far end of the building, similar-looking yellow barrels were stacked against the back wall. Each barrel had a Colossus Chemical Company label on it. Rex and Ivy could see the words "Flammable" and large black text spelling "CAUTION" on each barrel. The rest of the wording was too small to read from a distance. Whatever was in the barrels was being mixed into the compost through the watering system. The detectives worked their way closer, maneuvering through an opening in the fence. A loud cough from behind them startled the detectives. They turned.

"I'm sure Kevin will give you a tour when he returns," growled the young man from the front office. He led them back toward the front of the building.

"Thanks," said Rex. He wondered whether he should get a warrant for the next visit. But how could he justify the warrant?

"Next stop, office of PJ Moregone," announced Ivy as they slid into the police vehicle and pulled out of the SoilCycle Inc. yard.

Chapter 22

PJ MOREGONE

Thursday

Finding a parking spot near the building where the Hoopfest and Moregone Capital offices were located proved difficult. City workers had already started setting up "NO PARKING" signs on the core downtown streets in preparation of the coming event.

"As if parking wasn't hard enough downtown," mumbled Ivy. Complaining about parking downtown was part of the Spokane culture. Citizens would rather walk a few blocks than pay the high price for a space in one of the many lots sprinkled through the city center. The numerous parking lots did come in handy during Hoopfest though, considering a large percentage of youth division games were played on them.

The harried receptionist at the desk in the building's lobby put a call on hold while two other phone lines rang loudly and a man waited impatiently in front of the desk. A day before the big event and the Hoopfest office was jumping. The detectives hoped Moregone Capital would be quieter and they would finally get a chance to talk with its director and head accountant, PJ Moregone.

"How can I help you?" the receptionist asked pleasantly when she finally turned toward the two detectives.

"Is Mr. Moregone in his office this afternoon?" Rex asked.

"Yes, he is. Is he expecting you?"

"He might be, but we don't have an appointment, if that's what you mean."

"Let me just ring him."

"Don't bother. If you just point the way, we'll find him," said Rex.

"I don't know…"

But Ivy, who had noticed an office directional sign in the lobby, was already headed around a corner and Rex hurriedly caught up to her.

PJ Moregone's office was at the end of the hallway. The slightly ajar door allowed a harsh, whispered voice to float into the hall. Rex lifted a finger to his lips and he and Ivy tiptoed closer, stopping short of the door.

"…reporter… snooping around… why he wanted to talk to Director Hoozer. It's not like we're operating a … here! You… care of this…lay low… Can't have anyone… here." The phone clicked and the voice went quiet.

The two detectives listened to the sounds of a person pacing for a couple of minutes before they moved forward and knocked on the partially opened door.

"Come in," the harsh voice now called out loudly.

Rex pushed through the door to a dimly lit office with the blinds closed and smelling of cigarette smoke. Smoke curls ringed the head of PJ Moregone and drifted into the graying hair about his temples. Beady eyes bored through the thick lenses of his black-framed glasses at the two detectives. He wore a tailored dark suit and tie with a crisp, white shirt.

"Good afternoon, Mr. Moregone. Detectives Lizei and Begonia," said Ivy, showing her badge. She and Rex had agreed that Ivy would take the lead questioning the director of Moregone Capital.

Moregone snubbed out the cigarette in an ashtray sitting on the contemporary glass and metal desk before him. He reached out his hand in greeting. "What brings you here detectives?"

Ivy couldn't hide her surprise at seeing someone smoking in an office, especially someone who contracted with an organization involved with fitness. She stifled a cough and then said, "My condolences on the loss of your wife. It's a difficult time, I know, but we need to ask you a few routine questions."

"Does this mean you think her death wasn't an accident?" Moregone's stare challenged her. He kept his voice calm.

"A witness claims to have seen the accident that killed your wife and Jake Carville. She said a pickup truck ran the car off the bluff," Ivy answered.

Rex watched Moregone's face for a reaction. There was none. The detectives waited.

Finally, Moregone said, "I don't know why anyone would want to kill Jane. She had lots of friends. Everyone loved her."

"She was in the car with Jake Carville," pressed Ivy. She paused.

In a defensive voice, Moregone responded, "I've heard the rumors. They're not true. Jane was a major supporter of Mayor Prosciutto. She collaborated with Carville on the mayor's campaign. That's all."

Rex noticed Moregone's fists clenching and unclenching. "What can you tell us about the life insurance policy on Jane? Your insurance company told us that you raised the coverage recently. That looks a bit suspicious, wouldn't you agree?"

"Look, I didn't let you two in here to harass me and defame my wife," objected Moregone.

"Just routine questions," Ivy said calmly. "In these situations, we have to explore all possibilities, including family members."

"I've lost my wife and I'm busy with one of the city's largest events happening this weekend. I don't have time for your 'situations'."

"It only makes *your* situation worse to be uncooperative," said Rex. "The possibility of a cheating spouse and an increased insurance payout looks like a strong motive for murder. Where were you last Sunday?"

Moregone sighed, removed his glasses and pinched the bridge of his nose between his thumb and forefinger. "Home. Alone."

You stayed home while your wife went to an evening political fundraising event? Ivy wondered. She couldn't imagine Beau staying home while she socialized, unless he had to work. "Can anyone verify that you were home?"

"I was alone, so no. And if you'll excuse me…" Moregone picked up the receiver to the ringing phone on his desk. "Give me a minute," he said to whoever was on the other end of the line. "Next time, make an appointment and my lawyer can join us," he growled, turning back to Rex and Ivy and waving them toward the door.

"You might want to make your next call to your lawyer," Rex suggested.

"Do you think he was telling the truth?" Ivy asked her partner after they stepped out of the building into the summer heat.

"Even if he was, he's hiding something," Rex replied. "Did you notice how tense he was? And who was he discussing snooping reporters with on the phone when we first arrived?"

Chapter 23

STAKEOUT

Thursday Evening

"Sure. Conveniently, I don't have much of a social life," Ivy responded glumly when Rex proposed they work late that evening and return to SoilCycle Inc. It was already late afternoon when they pulled the unmarked police sedan into the parking lot at the Spokane Police Department headquarters.

"Something bugging you?" Rex turned to her with concern in his voice. It wasn't like Ivy to be morose. Usually, he wished for less loquaciousness, especially since she had a habit of initiating conversations before he had his third cup of coffee.

"I thought seeing somebody literally meant seeing them," said Ivy. "I see Yukon more than I see Beau."

"Yukon?"

"That's Beau's dog. I'm taking care of him while Beau is out of town. I shouldn't complain. Yukon is so sweet. Soft and cuddly. He's a great listener and he never argues. He likes to go for long walks together and is fiercely protective. He's everything a girl needs except romance."

"Since when did you need protecting? I've watched you throw men twice your size! Here all along, I thought you would protect me when we face down bad guys."

Ivy caught the twinkle in his eyes. Beneath that grouchy exterior, her partner had a compassionate heart. Before getting out of the vehicle, she gave him an affectionate punch to the shoulder. "Thanks, Boss."

As he exited his side of the sedan, Rex remarked, "If you two were married, you would spend more time together. Sure, you'd still both put in the hours at work, but all those small moments watering the plants, feeding the dog, brushing your teeth, etc. all add up."

Brushing teeth? Well, okay. Ivy could see his point. And Beau did have a smile that would make a dentist jealous. The thought of Beau made her smile.

Most of the day shift had left the office by the time the two detectives entered the building. They agreed to take a break and catch up on messages before returning to SoilCycle, Inc. Agents Bristol and Dyson were nowhere to be found. He and Ivy may as well be working on the case themselves, thought Rex.

Ivy had a voice message on her phone. Jill's boyfriend confirmed her account of the pickup truck on High Drive. After a cursory review of her email messages, Ivy did an online search for Kevin Greene and Mickey Gronk. Gronk didn't show up in her search. But Greene did.

Greene had a presence on several social media sites. His LinkedIn profile identified him as a former Marine, the current manager of SoilCycle, Inc. and having a B.S. degree in natural resources. He specialized in soils and organic chemistry. Greene appeared as a clean cut professional with sandy brown hair and blue eyes. He wore a long-sleeved, button-up shirt with the SoilCycle, Inc. logo.

Ivy found his other social media sites more revealing. On one, he posed in a brown T-shirt with the words "Compost Happens" across the chest. Marine insignias and lewd tattoos covered his muscular arms. His posts disclosed a young man passionate about his Second Amendment rights, partying and fast cars. And that's where Ivy found Mickey Gronk online — in party pictures posted on Greene's social media sites.

One picture in particular caught Ivy's attention. In the picture, Greene, Gronk and a couple of buddies appeared to be partying at a campsite in the woods. The posting identified Gronk as Gunk, the nickname Angela Marconi had used. Ivy recognized him as the corrections officer working with the crew at SoilCycle, Inc. She enlarged the picture on her computer. There on a camp table in the background sat crack pipes, roach clips and other drug paraphernalia.

"Ready?" Rex called from across the room.

"Just a minute. Let me print out a picture of Kevin Greene and Mickey Gronk. There's a connection there. The picture might come in handy," responded Ivy.

"On the way, let's swing by Red Pies. I've ordered us a Margherita pizza," said Rex. "This will be a vegetarian stakeout."

Ivy smiled. She was back to her cheerful self.

After picking up the pizza and locating a spot across the road from SoilCycle, Inc. where they could observe any activity without being noticed, the two detectives settled in for the wait. Fortunately, daylight lingered well into the evening this time of the year in the Lilac City and the heat dissipated as the sun lowered in the sky. Although he much preferred a proper table and chair and a glass of Chianti with his pizza, Rex admitted the pizza made it easier to forget he was in an undercover police car observing a commercial compost operation.

Only crumbs and a last bit of light in the day remained when Ivy pointed and whispered, "Look over there by that van."

Security lights on the office building spotlighted six men loading what looked like the chemical barrels the detectives had seen earlier in the day into a large, white van. Rex and Ivy counted eight barrels. One of the men appeared to be the young man who they spoke with at the SoilCycle office that afternoon. He and another man, who Ivy identified as Kevin Greene, directed the loading operation.

"Looks like Kevin is working overtime," Ivy remarked, while shooting a few pictures with a camera and zoom lens she brought for the stakeout. "Probably has trouble keeping a girlfriend," she muttered.

Three of the men wore prison uniforms. One beefy, thick-necked man with a shaved head looked to be a corrections officer. Based on Ivy's online research, it had to be Gronk. The machines, which earlier made so much noise, sat motionless and silent, creating an eerie sereneness as the men moved stealthily in the low light of dusk.

Once the barrels were in the van, Kevin Greene and his SoilCycle, Inc. assistant slid into the front of the vehicle. The others jumped into a second van and the two vehicles slowly edged along the driveway. Where the driveway intersected the road, the vans veered in opposite directions.

Ivy turned to Rex. "Which way, Boss?"

"Follow the van with the barrels. We need to find out what's in those containers."

At a distance, Ivy and Rex followed the van. They headed north toward the river. The van turned off the paved road and onto a narrow, gravel road surrounded by ponderosa pine trees. Ivy slowed to create more distance and checked the police vehicle's Global Positioning System to see where the road led. The road split eight miles ahead. The road to the right went toward an old, abandoned mine shaft near the river; the road to the left ended at a rock quarry.

"Let's pull off the road at the intersection," recommended Rex. "Unless they dump the barrels in the woods along the way, they're headed toward the quarry or the mine shaft. We'll wait and see which road they return from and then have the barrels retrieved tomorrow in the daylight."

Shortly before the intersection, Ivy drew over to the side of the road where a stubby pine tree and a clump of shrubs concealed the sedan from approaching vehicles. She turned off the headlights, noted the Global Positioning System, or GPS, coordinates and waited. Quiet settled for the next thirty-five minutes while the detectives retreated into their own thoughts.

"The mineshaft," cried out Rex, as a thundering cloud of dust came barreling past them from the right. Knowing the barrels likely wouldn't be disturbed, they noted the time and called it a day.

Chapter 24

AN INVITATION

Thursday Evening

As Rex neared his house that evening, porch lights in the neighborhood guided his Fiat along the street to his welcoming abode. On the stoop, clay pots spilling with lemon-yellow *Begonia tuberhybrida* made him feel at home. He missed the energy of his youth and he longed to unwind with an iced mocha on his patio beneath the stars. It had been a tiring day.

When he opened the door and turned on the light, a plain white envelope caught his attention. He didn't remember seeing it that morning. Someone had to have slipped the envelope beneath the door after he left the house. And it wasn't the mail carrier. She left posted mail in the red box that hung by the door.

Opening the envelope, Rex found the following message:

Begonia, I've done it! I have the proof. When the story publishes, it will be big! Pulitzer Prize level. But I need protection. They've been watching my house and the Lede building. I'm not sure who else to trust. I think they got Hoozer. Meet me at the Hoopfest Center Court at noon on Saturday. The crowd will provide cover.

Rex shook his head. Why didn't Rugula just come into police headquarters? In some ways, he could relate to Arthur Rugula. They were both in their late fifties, single and possessed a passion for plants. But Rex was much more sensible. If Rugula weren't so dramatic and grandstanding, maybe Rex could consider the garden reporter a friend.

The last place he wanted to meet Rugula was in a throng of thousands, especially in the mid-day heat. Besides, if anything went awry, people could get hurt. But he had no way to contact the reporter to change the plan. He would have to take his chances at Hoopfest.

Chapter 25

TEAMING UP

Friday

By the next day, the population of Spokane had swelled dramatically with people arriving to participate in the world's largest three-on-three basketball tournament. Hoteliers and restauranteurs were as gleeful as shop owners at Christmas. The "NO PARKING" signs throughout the downtown were in full force. Sporting good stores promoted all manner of basketball gear. The Lilac City had morphed into Hooptown, U.S.A.

Bristol and Dyson waited for Rex and Ivy in the office break room with a plate of fresh doughnuts and a pot of coffee. They seemed unusually cheerful and rose to meet Rex with friendly handshakes. The Spokane detective, who brought his own espresso into the room, wondered about their change in demeanor.

Ivy bounded into the room. She planned to leave early that afternoon to meet with Beau to pick up his team's registration packet for Hoopfest. Seeing the doughnuts, she asked, "Are we celebrating something?"

"We've hit a dead end," admitted Bristol after everyone was seated. "We're going to need your help."

"With?" asked Rex.

"We haven't found Agent Hoozer's notes or any of the evidence he gathered on the case. He was working with a local reporter—Arthur Rugula," said Dyson. "We haven't been able to connect with Mr. Rugula since we've been in town. It seems he's gone missing."

"We've been looking for him too," admitted Rex. "We might be able to help you but this has to be an equal partnership. We're still not sure what Henry Hoozer was investigating," the detective added.

Dyson shot Bristol a glance asking whether to proceed.

His partner nodded.

"Henry was an undercover agent investigating the Midwest company Colossus Chemical for other questionable dealings at the time the Environmental Protection Agency contacted the FBI for help. An anonymous tip to the EPA accused Colossus of illegally disposing a chemical called Defender. The FBI added the Defender complaint to Agent Hoozer's ongoing investigation of Colossus Chemical," explained Dyson.

"Defender is a long-lasting herbicide," added the agent. "It was used to control broadleaf weeds in lawns but banned from use with a few exceptions because it didn't break down when the lawn clippings were composted. It became a widespread problem when contaminated compost was used on gardens and small farms. Crops and plants died, causing hundreds of thousands of dollars in damage. Lawsuits ensued."

Rex decided to remain mum on the fact that he and Ivy had already discovered this much. "And yet, Defender is still sold on the market?"

Dyson continued, "Yes, although its use is limited. It can be applied on golf courses and pastures. The company that initially made Defender went bankrupt. Colossus Chemical acquired the company. To recoup its money, Colossus reduced the supply of the herbicide and raised the price. Supply and demand — basic economics. To limit supply, it had to dispose of the excess product, an expensive endeavor. No one knew what happened to all of the chemical that had already been produced."

"It's highly likely that someone associated with Colossus Chemical decided to end Henry's investigation, permanently," said Bristol. "Henry blew his cover after becoming Prosciutto's campaign manager. The company probably sicced their goons on him. Maybe they got Rugula too. I hope not because we have questions for him."

"It's a good theory," admitted Rex, "But I don't want to rule out other possibilities for the murder. We learned that the husband of Jane Moregone, the woman who was with Henry when he died, doubled the insurance coverage on his wife to a million dollars shortly before her death. Rumors pointed to a possible dalliance between Hoozer and Jane Moregone. PJ Moregone may have had a million and one reasons to kill his wife and Henry Hoozer was just collateral."

"We do know that Henry was using Mrs. Moregone to extract information about her husband," Dyson admitted. "We don't know the details but Henry found some financial connection between Colossus Chemical and Moregone."

"And then there's Mayor Prosciutto's political rivals," Rex continued. "The first campaign manager died in an eerily similar manner to Hoozer and Jane Moregone. All of the evidence indicated that Tip Seeborn's death resulted from an accident after a heavy night of drinking. Still, we could have missed something.

"Apparently, there's no love lost between candidate Phil Anders and Sammy Prosciutto. They've been competitors since college days when Anders beat Prosciutto in an election for school president. And then there was a romantic struggle between the two for the heart of Eve Pomme. Instead of becoming Mrs. Anders, Eve is now Mrs. Prosciutto and the two men are fierce political rivals. So far, I haven't found anything connecting candidate Tammy Hall to Prosciutto, other than the gubernatorial race.

"But if Henry Hoozer's death is tied to his investigation of Colossus Chemical, we'll have more answers after tomorrow. Arthur Rugula asked to meet me at noon Saturday in Riverfront Park," finished Rex.

"He did?!" Bristol practically shouted in his astonishment. "Isn't that where the three-on-three basketball tournament is happening? Won't there be crowds of people and all the streets shut down?" Bristol asked.

"Well, technically not all of the streets," answered Ivy, "But yes, many of the streets will be closed. Arthur Rugula has been hiding out in fear of his life and hopes the very public setting will provide an element of safety when he hands over his evidence."

"Okay, so, you've been in contact with Mr. Rugula already? Has he told you anything about the case?" asked Dyson.

Ivy told the two FBI agents about Rugula's USB drive, the newspaper clippings covering the plant mortality, and the Defender research. She also revealed that they had visited Manito Park, Near Nature Farm, the Airway Heights Corrections' community garden and finally SoilCycle, Inc. following Arthur Rugula's trail.

"That's another possibility," said Rex. "Our visit to Airway Heights

Correction Center and SoilCycle, Inc. unearthed a potential narcotics trafficking link between the two. We don't know yet whether Hoozer stumbled on the trafficking while investigating the Defender issue. There's a chance that whoever is responsible for the drug trafficking decided to knock off Hoozer."

"Sounds like you two have found more in a matter of days than what took Hoozer weeks to uncover," commented Bristol.

"Well, we did have Rugula's help," Ivy acknowledged.

"We'd like to meet this Mr. Rugula. Wonder why he hasn't called us back? We're the FBI," Bristol said, and then added, "What's the rendezvous plan for Rugula tomorrow? And why didn't he just send you the information? Why this big hoopla about meeting in the park?"

"You have to understand Arthur Rugula," responded Rex. "He knows us, so he trusts us. He tends to be extra protective of his sources. Plus, he wants to be noticed — has a flair for the dramatic. Believe me, I'd much rather he sent us all his evidence. By giving us his thumb drive, it's obvious he's scared of someone. Since he's been in hiding, we haven't been able to contact him. Communication has been only one-way.

"I want to bring the chief in on this," Rex continued. "He already planned for a larger than normal police presence at Hoopfest. I'm sure he'll be glad to accept the extra help from the FBI." The group stood and headed down the hallway toward Chief Blueblood's office.

As they approached the office, they saw the chief's nephew, Scout Blueblood, coming out the door. He carried a net bag full of basketballs in one hand and a gym bag in the other hand.

"Hey detectives," he greeted them with a big smile. "Big day tomorrow. Any of you playing?"

The first time Rex met the chief's nephew, Scout lay in a hospital bed in a coma. That encounter was the beginning of the Bloomsday Case a couple of years ago. He and Scout had both survived. Now Scout appeared fit and energetic. Rex felt old.

"I take it you mean Hoopfest," said Rex. "Sergeant O'Dendron's got a team. I'm deferring to the younger generation this year."

"Don't even look at me," said the height-challenged Ivy.

"Check out our team shirts. Uncle's bankrolling the team," said Scout as he pulled out a T-shirt and proudly held it for the detectives to see. *Rez Ball Legends* in light blue lettering spilled across the black shirt.

"Scout, this is FBI Agent Bristol and Agent Dyson. Agents, this is Scout Blueblood, Chief Barney Blueblood's nephew," said Rex, remembering his manners. He knew it wasn't just Scout's team. A basketball player and enthusiast, Chief Blueblood sponsored numerous Hoopfest youth teams from the Spokane Indian Reservation. It's the one good thing that came of boarding school, the chief often said about basketball.

"Maybe we'll see you on the courts. We'll be at the event," said Bristol. "We're here to talk with your uncle."

"Catch you later then," Scout said as he headed toward the building exit.

"What's that you want to discuss with me?" Chief Blueblood asked while opening the office door wider.

"Bristol and Dyson want to join our Hoopfest team," said Ivy.

"Henry's case evidence disappeared with his death. Our best option for solving this case appears to be the reporter Rugula," Bristol said. "Begonia, here, says there's a meeting planned with Rugula tomorrow in the park. We need to be part of that."

"Glad to see we're all on the same team," said the chief with a wink toward Rex. "Here's the game plan…"

Forty-five minutes later, the two FBI agents left the police station, followed by Rex, who had arranged to meet some of his colleagues and an undercover narcotics agent at the Hole-In-One Donut Shop.

Ivy had the rest of the day off and hurried to meet Beau at Riverfront Park. Finally, an afternoon together. Birds sang, flowers bloomed, the streets bustled with happy people. Bristol and Dyson were finally respecting her and Rex. They would all meet Arthur Rugula tomorrow and hoped to close the case. Life was good.

Chapter 26

SWEET STUFF

Late Friday Afternoon

The sweet smell of sugar combined with that of hot oil frying nearly gagged Rex when he entered the Hole-in-One Donut Shop, a favorite hangout for Spokane police and firefighters. The Hole-in-One earned top ratings in *Pastry Chef Magazine* and created serious addictions among doughnut connoisseurs in the Northwest, but Rex was a bit of an anomaly. He much preferred biscotti. He was only here to meet his colleagues for information.

He spied officers Scott "Hollywood" Pine and Stan Silva with a tough-looking young woman in dull brown dreadlocks sitting at a table in the far corner of the shop. They were keeping a low profile behind a plate stacked high with doughnuts.

"Hey Rex, have you met Mary Jane before?" asked Hollywood, when the homicide detective arrived at the table.

He recalled seeing Mary Jane during the Hoopfest briefing at headquarters but hadn't formally met her. "Agent Sativa, right? Are you new with the department?" asked Rex.

"Not really. I've been with the narcotics team for almost five years," she replied. "Most people call me Mary Jane. You've probably seen me at headquarters. I wear a lot of disguises, try to blend in, go unnoticed. And, I don't spend a lot of time here. The people I hang with usually order doughnuts to go."

Compared to the rest of the Spokane Police force, Mary Jane looked like a weed in a formal garden, observed the older detective. But having worked closely with Ivy the past few years, Rex wasn't about to underestimate the young woman.

"Hollywood tells me you've taken an interest in the Airway Heights Correction Center," she said. "What's the story?"

Rex appreciated that Mary Jane got right to the point. He followed suit. He told her about the meeting with Angela Marconi and the allegations that Mickey Gronk oversaw a drug trafficking operation in the prison. He wondered if the narcotics team had any knowledge of Gronk and his operations. He told her about the stakeout and the barrels of Defender herbicide, which had been recovered from the mineshaft by police officers and a hazardous substance team from the Department of Ecology earlier in the day. Rex also wanted to know if FBI Agent Henry Hoozer had worked with the narcotics team as part of his investigation.

"Mickey Gronk, huh? He's the corrections officer referred to as Gunk? Wicked dude! Yeah, for a few months now, we've suspected he's involved in drug trafficking. We just hadn't figured out how he's getting the drugs into the prison. Sounds like he has plenty of opportunity to move product along with the compost without being detected. I'll have to follow up with this Marconi gal," said Mary Jane.

"What about Hoozer? Did he contact you or anyone on your team?" Rex asked.

"The name's not familiar. Could he have gone by another name?"

"Carville," answered Rex. But he didn't know if Hoozer had any other aliases. Apparently Mary Jane had many.

"Nope," replied Mary Jane. "That's all I got. Hey, if you're not going to eat that doughnut in front of you, mind if I take it with me?"

Chapter 27

Pre-Game Party at O'Dendrens

Friday Evening

Shouts rang out from children scrimmaging beneath the hoop in the driveway as Rex arrived at the O'Dendren household for the pre-Hoopfest party. Phil had exaggerated about it being an estate, but with a household of seven, the O'Dendrens' home rivaled the Begonias' house in size. Cars lined the street. There must be a hundred people here, thought Rex. The neighbors will be calling the cops.

As usual, however, Sergeant Phil O'Dendren had invited the neighbors to the annual O'Dendren Hoopfest bash. Neighbors mingled with friends and family over burgers, beans and beers. Root beer for the kids. Tomorrow, this same crowd would be ball players, court monitors, scorekeepers and more.

"Watch me dunk," little Liam O'Dendren called out to Rex, who was walking into the yard. Liam zig-zagged across the driveway, dribbling past two male cousins. As he jumped toward the basket, his older sister Mary casually raised her arm, blocking the shot. "No fair," Liam shouted.

"Try the three-pointer," Rex encouraged Liam.

"How would you like your burger, Begonia?" Sergeant O'Dendren asked as Rex approached. With a spatula in one hand and tongs in another, O'Dendren stood in front of a Dagwood 1000 X-treme Professional Grill flipping hamburgers. "Drinks are in the cooler." He pointed the tongs toward a large ice chest near a picnic table and then turned back to directing two O'Dendren children who were ferrying plates of burgers and hot dogs to the table.

"This time of the year, he's constantly grilling and coaching,"

85

O'Dendren's wife Wendy laughed, while handing Rex a beer. "Are you on a team this year, Rex?"

"Not this time. With the high profile Hoopfest tournament happening downtown, the mayor plans to make an announcement. Chief Blueblood's ordered extra security. I'll be working." Rex was glad to have an excuse for opting out of competing, other than his aging knees.

"Well, we're thankful the chief made an exception for Phil."

"Did I hear you call me exceptional?" Sergeant O'Dendren asked his wife. "I won't argue with that."

"How's the O'Dendren team looking this year?" inquired Ivy, who along with Beau, had joined the growing crowd around the table laden with food.

"Which one? Between the kids and the relatives, we have one junior division team, three youth teams, a high-school team and, of course, two adult co-ed teams," Sergeant O'Dendren replied. "Mary grew two-inches this past year and she's got a mean lay-up. Her team could take the championship."

"Maybe she could teach me to shoot," said Ivy. "I'm feeling a bit out of my league with all this basketball talk."

"Hope you're a quick learner. We have our own slam-dunk and free-throw contests after dinner. Winners take home season tickets to the Gonzaga women's basketball games and a GU men's signed basketball," O'Dendren said.

"Wow! Those are some serious prizes," exclaimed Beau. "You'll have to compete against me," he said, giving Ivy a kiss on the cheek.

"Well if you win, you better use those tickets to take me to the games," she shot back, only half jokingly.

Daylight extended late into the evening in Spokane during June. After a short lesson from Mary, Ivy slipped away from the crowd and found a hoop in the neighbors' driveway. She decided with her short stature that her chances would be better in the free throw competition. She didn't have much basketball experience, but her many years of martial arts training and meditation taught her how to focus. Focus and aim, that's what mattered at the free throw line, right? When Sergeant O'Dendren announced the free throw contest, Ivy was ready.

One of the O'Dendren cousins won the slam dunk. It helps to be six-foot plus, thought Ivy. She stepped up to the free throw line. Each contestant had three warm up throws followed by one-minute to complete fifteen shots. The younger players shot ten feet from the basket, while the older players stood fifteen feet away from the hoop. The person sinking the most of fifteen baskets won, with a shoot-off in case of a tie. Ivy was the second to the last contestant. A neighbor led with twelve baskets.

Ivy closed her eyes and entered her Zen mode. When she opened them again, all she could see was the ball in front of her face and the basket hanging from the backboard. She shot eleven straight before missing the twelfth shot. She made the next two and threw wide when a siren in the background broke her concentration.

Mary O'Dendren was the last contestant. She quickly tossed eleven baskets and then missed one, just like Ivy had. The ball easily swished through the net on the next throw. It came down to the last two shots. She hit the rim. The pressure rose. The ball sank, just missing the basket.

Ivy didn't know whether to feel elated for winning or terrible for beating her mentor.

"Woohoo, you did it!" shouted Beau.

Ivy looked at Mary, who grinned and said, "You can be on my team any day! And no worries. Dad takes us to all to the GU games anyway."

The evening wound down. Rex left to check in on the Begonia family, who were also fielding multiple Hoopfest teams and preparing for the big day.

Before everyone left, Sergeant O'Dendren reminded people to pack lots of sunscreen and Gatorade the next day. "It's going to be a scorcher!"

As they left, Beau turned to Ivy and said, "Hey Superstar, let's stop at The Palisades before going home. I owe you an uninterrupted sunset."

Fifteen minutes later, they sat on the basalt rocks watching the fading golden light reflect off the city's buildings, casting the downtown in an orange glow. They had not sat here since the evening of Tip Seeborn's demise. The events of the past couple of weeks made it seem like ages ago.

Ivy stared out at the horizon viewing the city whose citizens she had taken an oath to protect. She reflected on her struggle to gain confidence and earn respect on the male-dominated police force. She thought about the long and abnormal hours of her demanding job. She also considered the satisfaction of putting criminals behind bars. Okay, so maybe it wasn't as lauded as keeping the streets' potholes filled, but keeping Spokane's streets safe needed superheroes too. But where did Beau fit in? She turned to look at him.

Beau had been watching her. He took Ivy's hand in his and said, "I know these past few months have been difficult. We've both been so busy. That's probably not going to change. But it did get me thinking…" and with his other hand, he pulled a small box out of his pocket and gave it to Ivy. "…I'd like us to be together. I love you Ivy Lizei. Will you marry me?"

Ivy opened the box and looked at the ring — a small diamond flanked by two emeralds that matched her green eyes — and then gazed into Beau's deep brown eyes. It felt like all the world melted around them and they were the only two beings left. And then… oh yeah, it's 93 degrees still and she was sweating. For once Ivy was speechless, so she gave him a tearful nod and wrapped her arms around Beau's neck. She planted a sweaty kiss on his lips, hoping it was answer enough for now.

After the tears subsided, they sat together and watched the stars appear in the sky.

Finally, Ivy laughed. "Yes, it's yes," she said.

"Good," Beau replied kissing her again. "I don't think Yukon would let me back in the house if you had said 'no'."

For the next hour, they snuggled beneath the stars, sometimes in silence and sometimes talking about the future. Ivy felt the happiest she ever had. She didn't have to prove herself. Beau loved her just the way she was. She knew that they still faced challenges melding their demanding lives, but they would figure it out together.

Finally, Ivy said, "I hate to call it a night, but in the near future you have a big game and I have a murder to solve."

Chapter 28

THE HEAT IS ON

Saturday Morning

Temperatures had already reached the high 70s by the time Rex arrived at Cafe Noir to jump start his day. During the morning news, KRUM-TV weather forecaster Misty Mourne predicted a record-breaking 106-degrees for the day. In addition to the larger than normal police presence at Hoopfest, the mayor had ordered extra EMTs to be on hand in anticipation of heat stroke and exhaustion. Rex ordered a tall, triple-shot, iced Americano.

"You sure that will be strong enough?" asked Gina, the raven-haired barista who came close to sainthood as far as Rex was concerned. In a city of award-winning baristas, Gina's espresso drinks were heavenly. Father O'Malley, from St. Ignatius Church across the street, concurred.

"If you're headed downtown for the games, you'll be needing a thermos of the fortified stuff in this heat," Father O'Malley chimed in after joining Rex at a table.

"Thanks Father. Will you be going to Hoopfest today?"

"Aye. Quite a few of the parishioners are on teams. I have a few greenbacks wagered and I'll be there to provide divine intercession on my parishioners' behalf."

"O'Dendrens?"

"But of course," chuckled Father O'Malley. "I'm not sure if Phil and Wendy have raised a family or a basketball team. Mary O'Dendren led St. Ignatius to State this year. Her team is the *Four Leaf Clovers*. They'll be channeling the luck o' the Irish. If you go downtown, you can watch them at the high school elite section of Center Court. Look for me in the shade."

Downtown, spectators hauled coolers, camp chairs and colorful umbrellas to set up along the courts, which had sprung up like mushrooms overnight thanks to many volunteers. At the plaza in Riverfront Park, the last of the teams checked in and others made final player changes. Hoopfest officials readied for the opening ceremonies at Center Court. Tip-off was scheduled for 8:00 a.m. on all 400 plus courts.

Rex parked north of Riverfront Park. A riot of color from the mural covering the new 10,000-square foot basketball court greeted him when he walked into the park. Now divided into half courts where teams practiced in anticipation of tipoff, the paint had dried on the new playing surface just days before the start of Hoopfest.

Once again, Sammy Prosciutto had proven to be the can-do politician. The mayor wasn't the only one benefiting from the expanded sports area. Rex's "homework" delving into PJ Moregone had revealed that the accountant profited financially from the city contract for the court. Moregone's backdoor financial moves were out of bounds. If by the end of the day, Rex didn't arrest him for the death of Henry Hoozer and Jane Moregone, he'd at least see the man in judicial court for his financial crimes.

By now, Rex had approached Center Court, located inside the Pavilion, at the heart of Riverfront Park. The park spanned the Spokane River running through the center of the city. Altogether, the elaborate network of temporary basketball courts occupied 45 municipal blocks, spreading out from the park on both sides of the river. Two basketball hoops stood back-to-back, each with its own half court, score keeper with table, and court monitor. Spectators began to fill the narrow strips of street and sidewalk beside the half courts until the downtown resembled a large-scaled version of a brightly-colored ant hill.

Rex planned to look for Arthur Rugula by posting himself just west of Center Court between the tent where teams checked in and the large master scoreboard where official tournament results would be posted. Ivy and agents Bristol and Dyson would mingle near the exhibitor booths across the plaza but within sight of Rex. Already, additional police officers worked security throughout the park and the surrounding Hoopfest area.

Chief Blueblood had planned for all contingencies with the exception of blistering heat, thought Rex. Even though it was early in the day, he tried to stay in the shade while making his way through the crowd toward Center Court. Why had Arugula chosen a noon meeting, in the heat of the day? Rex had arrived early to spot anyone looking suspicious and who might harm Arthur Rugula.

By 11 a.m., temperatures had risen to 96 degrees Fahrenheit and the light hoodie he wore to conceal his weapon caused Rex to sweat. The smell of Gatorade and sunscreen filled the air. Most of the people around him wore as little clothing as decently possible. So much for being undercover thought Spokane's top detective.

As he passed the Clock Tower, Rex recognized a woman with dreadlocks dribbling a basketball. She and her teammates all wore tank tops emblazoned with pictures of a cannabis leaf and the name *High Nooner*s. It was Mary Jane. At least one of them was undercover.

In addition to being the world's largest three-on-three basketball tournament, Hoopfest seemed to have a boundless display of a different type of pick-up behavior, grown out of neighborhood pickup basketball games. Young men and women showed off their athletic prowess and flaunted their physical charms as they attempted to attract each other. Pheromones flew. Rex hadn't seen so much flirting since high school. More than one kind of courting took place on Hooptown U.S.A.'s streets, he observed.

Men dominated the senior division. Rex recognized Judge Rudy Marconi playing on a team with the name *Supreme Court* on its T-shirts. Rex overheard one grizzled, but fit, player boasting this was his seventeenth year of playing at Hoopfest. The sound of balls bouncing on the pavement and the banter of players reminded the detective of his youth. If he could just get back in shape, maybe that would help win over Molly Murrow.

The Hoopsters, a team of octogenarian women wearing hoop skirts with their jerseys, proved the game wasn't just for men or youth. The youngest players palled around with their buddies, excited to participate in a sport alongside older kids and adults. Three second-graders wearing *Tater Shots* uniforms and braids ran across Rex's path.

"Hey Detective!" yelled a fit, young man dribbling on the next court that Rex passed. It was Nate Nettle, the farmer from Near Nature Farms. He and his sister Natalie played on a co-ed team.

Rex waved and chuckled. The team's green T-shirts sported the name *Lettuce Bee Champs*. Rex recognized the young farmers' opponents as a team of Spokane firefighters. They wore red shirts with *Great Balls of Fire* blazoned across the front.

The detective crossed the footbridge, spied Ivy near the exhibit booths and strolled by the VIP stage. Mayor Prosciutto commanded a prominent place on the shaded stage where he watched the elite game being played on the Center Court. Hoopfest Director Hal Hoozier, the Gonzaga and Eastern Washington University coaches, and various local VIPs sat with him. KRUM-TV sportscaster Duncan Wilson and Molly Murrow covered the action at Center Court. Molly was interviewing former Gonzaga player and NBA all-star Chuck Taylor in front of a camera. Did Rex detect an admiring look on Molly's face?

He circled back toward the master scoreboard to meet up with Rugula and pretended to look for information. He glanced at his Bvlgari watch. Five minutes until noon. He looked toward the plaza. No sign of Rugula yet. Thirty feet from the scoreboard, two teams battled on the high school elite section of Center Court. The *Four Leaf Clovers* tied the game. Rex saw Phil O'Dendren yelling and screaming on the sidelines.

Noon. Still no indication of Rugula. At 12:05 p.m. Rex grew concerned. Mary O'Dendren heaved a three-point shot to win the game.

Chapter 29

SHOOTOUT ON THE COURTS

Saturday Afternoon

Rex finally spotted Arthur Rugula. The slight reporter with thick glasses and thinning white hair hurried furtively toward the detective, slowing only to glance occasionally over his scrawny shoulders. He wore a white, short-sleeved, button-up shirt, brown trousers and a skinny striped tie. To a basketball tournament! Rugula certainly wasn't a candidate for undercover work thought Rex, but who was he to judge?

Rugula stopped in front of the scoreboard near the detective. His back faced Rex. "Thanks for coming," he whispered hoarsely. "I have the final evidence. Henry Hoozer was so close, but they killed him."

"Who? Who killed Hoozer?"

A shot rang out from the edge of the Pavilion. The shooter's movement caught Rex's attention. Immediately, he leaped toward Rugula, knocking the reporter to the ground. A second shot quickly followed. Pain exploded in Rex's leg. Within seconds, he was sprawled on the ground, grabbing his knee.

Chaos ensued. Screams filled the air. Players, spectators and Hoopfest volunteers ran in all directions. Basketballs rolled, bounced and tripped people as they fled. Parents grabbed children. The shrill sound of a court monitor's whistle sent a warning. Police officers rushed toward Center Court.

Ivy ran toward the shooter with her gun drawn, yelling at him to drop his weapon. She recognized the stocky man with a shaved head from the Airway Heights Corrections Center — Mickey Gronk.

Gronk raised his gun and aimed at Ivy. At that moment, a basketball flew through the air. Thunk! The ball smacked the gunman forcefully on his right temple. Gronk crumpled to the ground.

"Slam dunk!" shouted Sergeant O'Dendren, raising his arms to celebrate his shot.

Ivy quickly apprehended the culprit and handcuffed his arms behind his back. "Thanks for the assist, Phil. Looks like this guy's out of the game. Would you take him in? I've got to check on Rex."

But Father O'Malley, who had been watching the elite high school basketball game, had already reached Rex's side.

"Do you need…"

"I'm not done yet, Father. Just get an EMT." Rex grimaced and held a hand over his leg trying to staunch the bleeding.

"Y-y-y-you saved me," squeaked Arthur Rugula trying to get up from his knees.

"Rex! Rex! Please tell me you're okay," pleaded Ivy, hurrying back to where her partner lie sprawled on the hot concrete. She dropped to his side and reached out to him.

He groaned.

Agents Bristol and Dyson appeared, followed by an Emergency Medical Technician and the KRUM-TV reporters. Police officers were already cordoning off the scene. Molly tried to get to Rex but a young police officer blocked her path.

"Sorry, nobody past the barricades. Even the press," the officer declared.

"Rex!" called out Molly.

"Sorry, miss. It's a crime scene," said the officer.

The EMT ordered everyone to step back away from the injured detective. He set down his medical kit and turned to Rex. "There's an ambulance on its way. While we're waiting, let's get a look at this," he said, cutting the pant leg to access the wound. "It might hurt a little."

"Only a little?!" Rex grimaced. This had to be worse than anything Chuck Taylor endured on the court. He saw Molly and Duncan Wilson with the KRUM-TV camera a few feet away, on the other side of the police barricade. Dread crossed Molly's face. Rex tried to appear stoic.

After a cursory examination of Rex, the EMT handed Father O'Malley a pair of latex gloves and showed him how to apply pressure with gauze on Rex's wound, while he checked the detective's vital signs. "Hold it down tight. It doesn't matter if he screams. We've got to slow down that blood flow," instructed the EMT.

"Augh!" yelled Rex as Father O'Malley pressed. "Is this my penance?"

The EMT turned to Rugula next.

But Bristol was glaring at the shaking reporter. "Where's the evidence?" The FBI agent demanded.

"The -th-th-there were two shooters," Rugula whimpered before collapsing.

Ivy, Bristol and Dyson looked at each other. A second shooter? Where? Thousands of people still filled the park.

"Hey, ease up. I need to treat this guy for shock and we have to get them both out of here," the EMT, aiding Rugula, declared to Bristol as the ambulance arrived. It drove up on the pathway and came to a stop by the barricade.

"I'm coming with you," Agent Dyson announced. He wasn't letting Rugula disappear again.

Rex felt dizzy. Faces blurred, voices slurred. Everything seemed to happen in slow motion but he knew only a few moments had passed since the shooting. The last voice he heard before passing out was that of Molly Murrow, reporting live from Riverfront Park where a law enforcement officer had been shot and a shooter apprehended.

Molly, and the thousands of Hoopfest attendees, had not yet heard that the game was far from over — a second shooter was on the loose at Hoopfest.

Chapter 30

HOOPFEST HOSTAGE

Saturday Afternoon

A commotion erupted near the VIP stage. Shouts and screams rose. The crowd moved as if the earth were shaking.

After putting Sergeant O'Dendren in charge of the apprehended shooter and watching Rex and Rugula carried off toward the hospital, Ivy raced toward the VIP stage. Agent Bristol quickly followed. They encountered a wave of panicked people.

Ivy stopped abruptly when she saw the stage. Instantly, she recognized SoilCycle Manager Kevin Greene. He stood on the stage holding an FNX-45 Tactical handgun to Mayor Sammy Prosciutto's head. He held the mayor's twisted arm behind Prosciutto's back and clutched the mayor close to him. If anyone tried to shoot Greene, Kevin could immediately dispatch Sammy Prosciutto. Ivy had seen the mayor look terrifying but never terrified. He looked terrified now.

"Everyone just stay back and no one will get hurt," Greene shouted.

FBI Agent Bristol arrived at that moment with his gun drawn. "It's no use Greene. We have the park surrounded," he yelled.

"Yeah? I think Mr. Mayor here will get me through your police line," retorted Greene, yanking the mayor's arm while keeping the barrel of the gun to the mayor's head. "No one wants to see the boss get hurt." He started pulling the mayor away from Center Court and out of the Pavilion.

Sirens sounded in the distance. The wave of people flowed outward into the perimeters of the park. Still, plenty of people occupied the park. Greene and the mayor slipped into the wave. The crowd noise and focus on the games slowed the realization of the present danger. Police officers attempted to disperse the crowds while police SWAT members sought strategic locations to target Greene without incurring collateral damage.

Out of the corner of her eye, Ivy spied a small drone following Greene and Mayor Prosciutto from a distance. Chief Blueblood had added the drone to the security plan upon Ivy's recommendation. She was thankful that he had. They couldn't risk a shootout in this crowd and Greene probably knew it. Did he have a vehicle waiting for him? Ivy wondered. If so, it must be blocks away due to the road closures. Surely, they would have an opportunity to get Greene before he could get away.

If he crossed the river on the narrow footbridge near the Clock Tower, the SWAT members could trap Greene from both sides. But, the mayor being a hostage was problematic. Ivy knew what Rex would say about that — "not the first time the mayor was problematic." Her partner often questioned whether the mayor overstepped legal lines in pursuit of power. But Ivy knew Rex wouldn't want the mayor harmed.

Greene veered from the Clock Tower and slipped between the food tents set up on the wider, still crowded, footbridge. Ivy lost sight of him as he and the mayor blended into the mass of people. The drone would have to take over.

Ivy clicked on her two-way radio. "Chief, Agent Lizei here. Do you copy?"

"Affirmative Lizei. What's your location and status?"

"I'm in the park. Approaching the north side of the footbridge where the food vendors are set up. The perp's disappeared into the crowd. He was last seen near the food tents, heading south on the bridge. I need your aerial eyes to help track him."

"10-4. I'm on it."

Agent Bristol, who also tailed Greene, lost him too. His voice came across the radio. "Bristol here. I'm nearing the bridge now. Can we cut him off on the south end of the park?"

"Negative," came Chief Blueblood's voice over the radio. "Greene's already crossed the bridge and is exiting the park. I'm sending the SWAT team in that direction."

The chief watched the action beside a drone technician in the incident command center. On any other day, he could see the south edge of the park from where he sat in the command center, hastily set up inside City Hall. Despite the location being across the street from the park, a swarm of Hoopfest attendees blocked his view better than Chuck Taylor blocking a lay-up.

The radio crackled. "Perpetrator in sight. We're closing in," Ivy heard the SWAT team captain relay. "Perp's entering O'Donovan's Pub from the back." Oh no, the pub would be crawling with people during Hoopfest, she thought. Had they heard about the shooter? Had they evacuated?

They did now. Patrons poured out of the pub quicker than Guinness on St. Patrick's Day. SWAT members surrounded the building and swept pub patrons across the street where a police barrier was being set up hurriedly. Ivy recognized Ryan, the friendly young bartender, from earlier visits to the pub. Ryan guided a man screaming hysterically. The man's eyes bulged. Blood streamed between his fingers as he held his head in one hand and leaned on Ryan with the other.

"What happened?" asked Ivy, coming to a stop and catching her breath when she neared Ryan and the man she guessed to be O'Donovan's cook, based on his apron and clothing. Agent Bristol and a member of the SWAT team joined them.

"Some guy with a gun burst through the back door and into the kitchen," Ryan answered. "He beaned Stu, here, with a gun, then disappeared down the stairs."

Ivy radioed for an EMT and then turned back to Ryan. "Was the guy with the gun alone?"

"No, some other guy was with him but I only saw the one gun. It looked like the first guy was dragging the second guy with him."

"Where do the stairs lead?"

"It's a basement storage area," explained the bartender, "but it's connected to the tunnel system under the city."

"A tunnel system?" Ivy was surprised. She was unaware of any tunnels beneath Spokane. Few Spokanites were. "If they enter a tunnel system, we could lose them. We need to hurry before they reach those tunnels," she urged.

"Too late for that," said Ryan, but Ivy was already racing down the stairs. Bristol and the SWAT team members ran close behind.

A hefty steel door at the bottom of the stairs stopped their progress. The largest of the SWAT members pushed against the door to no avail.

"He must've blocked it from the other side," declared SWAT Team Captain Gunner Gowan. "If they're in the tunnels, they could surface in any number of locations. Let's get back upstairs and find a map, or someone who knows the layout of the tunnel system."

Great, Ivy thought bitterly. The search just grew citywide and every minute mattered.

Chapter 31

A TUNNEL OF LIGHT

Saturday Afternoon

Rex regained consciousness while lying on a gurney being wheeled into Holy Heart Hospital. His surroundings looked fuzzy but his prominent Roman nose picked up a sharp, sterile hospital scent and he could hear the EMTs and emergency room staff. He tried to speak, but could only manage a grunt. He had no sense of time.

"He's lost a lot of blood… blood pressure's down to 60. Pulse is 115… two units… negative blood."

"…cross-match … order six units…electrolytes… prep to operate…"

Rex's eyes opened enough to see a group of people in surgical gowns and masks hovering above him. Behind them, an overhead surgical lamp shone brightly causing him to blink. An IV was hooked up to his right arm. He felt a sharp prick in his left arm. He blinked once more and then the last memory he had was of a dark tunnel leading toward a bright light.

Chapter 32

Mapping a Strategy

Saturday Afternoon

While Rex underwent surgery, Ivy and Agent Bristol went under the city.

The hunt for Greene and Mayor Prosciutto began above ground with the police shutting down the streets and Hoopfest courts. Beneath the streets and sidewalks of Hooptown U.S.A. lay a labyrinth of concrete tunnels dating back to 1890, when the city piped water from the Spokane River to the downtown Steam Plant. The plant then pumped steam through pipes in the tunnels to heat many of the commercial buildings in the city center. Later, during the prohibition era and after the buildings had their own heating systems, portions of the tunnels housed speakeasies beneath legitimate businesses. Now, brick walls closed off many of the tunnels, which dead-ended in the unlikeliest of places.

It had taken almost an hour for the Spokane Police Department to track down a city public works employee who could locate an up-to-date map of the city's underground tunnels. Chief Blueblood, Ivy, Agent Bristol and SWAT Team Captain Gowan stood over the map, which was spread out on a table in the City Hall incident command center. A maze of lines on the map represented miles of tunnels snaking beneath Spokane's streets like arteries throughout a body.

Just then, the mayor's older brothers Frankie, Sal and Fast Eddie burst into the room shouting that they could enter the tunnels, extricate their little brother and deal with the perpetrator.

"Chief! You've gotta let us in there," Fast Eddie shouted. "We can get Sammy out and take care a' that creep."

"Whoa! Slow down," responded the chief, hoisting his hand in the air

101

like a crossing guard. He recognized the mayor's brothers from their work on city contracts. He raised a wary eyebrow. "What are you guys talking about?"

Sal slapped his brother on the back. "Frankie, here, heard on the dispatch radio that Sammy's been taken hostage under the city. That's when Frankie called me and Fast Eddie. We can get him out," proclaimed Sal.

"Yeah, an' we can deal with the bozo that nabbed him," added Fast Eddie, punching the fist of his right hand into the palm of his left one.

"How did you knuckleheads even get in here?" Chief Blueblood asked rhetorically, his neck turning purple and his eyes glaring. "We need to rescue the mayor as quickly as possible, but I don't want to send anyone into the tunnels until we know what we are dealing with," he explained, "And, if anyone goes in, it will be our officers."

"We know those tunnels like they're our backyard," said Frankie. "Nonno — that's our grandad — did a lot of business there back in the day. Took us through all the tunnels when we were kids. You should hear the stories he told. Lively times during prohibition. But not everybody that went down there, came back up, if you know what I mean. Them tunnels are haunted. Leave it to us. We can get Sammy out."

"I won't put civilians in harms way," countered the chief. "Besides, doesn't Kevin Greene work for you at SoilCycle, Inc., Sal?" How do I know you two aren't in cahoots?"

"What's Greene got to do with it?" asked Sal.

"Greene's the guy that has Sammy," responded the chief.

"Greene's an employee, if that's what you mean. But he isn't working for me in the way you're implying," insisted Sal Prosciutto. "I wouldn't be involved in anything to soil the family reputation, not with Sammy running for Governor."

And when he's not running for governor? wondered Ivy, her eyes rolling.

"Maybe you can help us with Greene. Does he have any family? Wife or girlfriend?" asked Chief Blueblood. He was already anticipating hostage negotiations.

"Nah, he doesn't have anybody close," replied Sal Prosciutto. "Bit of a loner. Nothing to lose. Makes him more dangerous."

"Fortunately it appears the perp chose a tunnel that's been blocked. He can't get far," Gowan declared, pointing to the city block under O'Donovan's Pub. That's where he had stationed the rest of his team.

"It's too risky to send many people down there. Lots of opportunity for ambush or the mayor to get hurt," explained Gowan. "Our best bet is to flush him out and nab him when he exits. We'll have to send in a small team. We can't risk using tear gas as long as he has the mayor."

The SWAT captain and Chief Blueblood chose Ivy, Agent Bristol and two SWAT members to enter the tunnel beneath O'Donovan's Pub. Captain Gowan ordered the rest of the SWAT team members to guard the tunnel entrances of the passageways connecting to the pub.

Ivy studied the map. Already, the adrenaline helped her focus. She committed the visual to memory. It looked like the tunnel beneath O'Donovan's stretched beneath the buildings to the west and south for approximately a block before being sealed. At various places, the tunnels widened into rooms. In addition to access from O'Donovan's Pub, the section of tunnel underneath the pub could be reached from two other nearby businesses: Scout & Finches Toy Store and the Mocking Bird Mug Coffee House. Locked metal doors separated the passageways beneath the businesses.

Gowan decided the group would enter from the coffee shop. A half hour ticked by as the team waited for the owner of the Mocking Bird Mug to show up with a key to the tunnels beneath the shop.

Chief Blueblood finally convinced the Prosciutto brothers to leave. The search team reviewed the map, checked their gear and readied for the assault on the tunnels.

"Everyone have your bullet resistant vests and helmets?" asked Gowan. He handed extra helmets to Ivy and Agent Bristol, who wore the vests but typically not helmets. He made sure everyone in the group had night-vision goggles. "Your radios may not work underground in some of the tunnels. But these goggles will give you an advantage in the darkness."

Already, sweat trickled down Ivy's forehead. The additional gear only intensified how hot she felt. Drat this heat. Ivy felt like she was wilting. Or was it nerves? Were the others nervous? She knew that a search operation posed elevated danger to law enforcement officers. Greene still had plenty of places to hide. And he was an armed ex-marine. With a hostage.

Chapter 33

A DARK TUNNEL

Saturday Afternoon

A dank musty smell slammed Ivy's nose as soon as the door opened to the basement of the coffee house. At least the air felt cooler!

The search team waited a few moments before stepping onto the stairs. If Greene was below in this part of the tunnel system, he would see them due to the light in the room behind them. A quiet set in. Adrenaline kicked in.

The first SWAT member took a step forward. Nothing. The next followed. Then Bristol. Finally Ivy. The door quickly shut, enveloping them in darkness except for the eerie green light created by the night goggles.

Were the stories of a haunted underground Spokane real? It sure felt eerie. The spooky lighting distorted movement and softened the outlines of bodies. Ivy could easily imagine her colleagues as apparitions floating silently through the gloom. The green glow offered just enough light to maneuver down the stairs and into the passageway.

Ivy ran a hand along the cold, concrete wall as she inched forward. Only a few moments ago, she had been sweating. Now, goose bumps rose on her arms. All was quiet except — drip. Drip. Drip. Where was the water coming from? Then from behind her — a knocking sound.

She turned quickly. It was just the pipes. She shivered. Her heart pounded. Her breath quickened. Darkness and adrenaline heightened all of her senses.

The passage turned right and then opened into a small room. Ivy scanned the room left to right. An ornate, wooden bar, tucked in a corner, must have dated back to the early twentieth century and prohibition days.

An area to the side looked like it could have been a stage with a small dance floor. For a split second, her concentration broke. Ivy imagined Spokanites in suits and flapper dresses shimmying across the floor. Maybe she and Beau… Stay focused.

The passage narrowed again. They must be nearing the area under the toy store. Dust kicked up from the team's movement caused Ivy to muffle a sneeze. She froze. Despite her attempt to be silent, every motion, every action sounded amplified in the underground labyrinth. She could hear her heart beating!

The lead SWAT member turned another corner as the second team member covered him. Seconds passed. Then minutes. What was happening up ahead? wondered Ivy. Why was it taking so long?

A gentle movement tickled her left wrist. She reached across to her wrist with her right hand, still gripping the gun and looked down — a recluse spider! It was larger than the ones she had seen in her dad's greenhouses.

A shot rang out. Then more shots.

Chapter 34

SHOOTOUT IN THE DEPTHS

Saturday Afternoon

"You could have accidentally pulled the trigger," Ivy silently reprimanded herself after flinging the spider aside.

Bristol was first to react to the shots heard coming from the room where the SWAT team members had entered. He picked up a chair from along the concrete wall and tossed it through the doorway into the room. Another shot reverberated, and then a scuffling sound followed.

After recovering her senses, Ivy aimed her gun toward the doorway. She heard running footsteps echoing off the concrete walls. The rhythm suggested two people. At least one must be limping, she surmised.

She and Bristol quickly entered the next room, staying low to the ground. The trick of throwing a chair in ahead of them to draw fire could only work once.

Kegs lining one wall indicated that they were under O'Donovan's Pub. Pipes hung from the ceiling and along another wall in multiple directions. Water blasted out of an open pipe. One of the SWAT members lay on the floor in a pool of water mixed with blood. The other sat propped against a wall, holding his arm. A stray bullet, or bullets, must have opened the pipe, spraying water and catching the SWAT members off guard, giving Greene an advantage.

Bristol called out, "Give it up Greene. We've surrounded the place. You'll never make it out alive."

Ivy hid behind a maze of pipes and surveyed the concrete room. For once, she was thankful for her small size. She inched forward, staying behind the pipes. Bristol stood behind shelves on the other side of the room.

"If I don't, he doesn't." Greene pulled Mayor Prosciutto closer.

"He's injured," yelled the mayor. Greene hit him across the face with the back of his gun. The mayor let out a rasping cry. Then, "I – I – I'm sure we can work something out. Just let me go," he pleaded, facing his captor.

"Shut up," Greene snapped, then turned toward his pursuers. "Call off the cops. At all the tunnel entrances."

"We would but the radios don't work down here," Bristol replied.

"This is the 21st Century. Use a phone," snarled Greene. "Put it on speaker and Mr. Mayor here can tell your boss what to do, if he knows what's good for him."

Greene must think Bristol is a city detective answering to Chief Blueblood, thought Ivy. And, if I'm lucky, he assumes Bristol is alone now. If the FBI agent could keep him talking, maybe I could maneuver around and catch Greene off guard. She signaled to Bristol, hoping he understood her attempt at pantomime. He must have because he launched into a rambling discourse.

"Sorry buddy, nada signal; no bars down here," said Bristol, leaning against a keg. "We'll get you out of here, but first I want to know why you tried to kill the reporter, Arthur Rugula. Was he onto your Defender scheme with Colossus Chemical? Was he next on your hit list after Jake Carville?" He paused for an answer but when none came, he continued, "Who ran Carville off the road — you, or your pal Mickey Gronk?"

"How stupid do you think I am?" Greene finally retorted. "Criminals only open up to the cops in movies. I'm not telling you nuthin."

Definitely stupid, thought Ivy as she inched her way close to Greene while staying behind the pipes. Only a few more feet and she would have a clear shot at him.

Bristol shifted his weight. As he did so, his left foot bumped into a pile of debris.

The sound made the gunman jumpy. He fired toward the noise, hitting Bristol.

Ivy caught her breath. The dirtbag just didn't miss! How many more bullets did he have? she wondered. Despite the chilliness underground, she was sweating again.

"I know you're still out there. I can hear you," Greene hissed. "But don't you worry. I have plenty of ammu…."

Just then, a flash of light appeared momentarily above and behind Greene, catching him off guard. A thundering noise followed.

Mayor Prosciutto used the moment of distraction to yank away from his captor. He flung himself onto the floor beside a pile of boxes just as a beer keg barreled down a metal track from above them. The keg grazed Kevin Greene, knocking the gun out of his hand.

Ivy saw her opportunity. She leapt from behind the shelves, quickly holstered her own weapon and reached for Greene. Before he could tell what was happening, Ivy grabbed his arm while simultaneously kicking her leg forward, then brought it back behind his knee. The judo move landed the surprised crook on the stone, cold floor. Before he could reach for his gun, he was on his stomach and handcuffed with his hands behind his back.

"Constant movement, proper body position and a sense of timing," Ivy declared.

Greene glared at Ivy and erupted in a string of curses.

Agent Bristol groaned.

"Are you okay?" Ivy asked him while keeping an eye on Greene.

"Just a little shaken," answered Mayor Prosciutto, who stood holding Greene's gun.

Chapter 35

NEVER BETTER

Saturday Evening

Rex woke in a hospital bed. He felt groggy from surgery. His eyelids were heavy. He fell back asleep. Later, he woke again and blinked. He looked at his left leg, wrapped and set, then glanced at his arm hooked to an IV. The pain meds must be strong he thought. He didn't feel a thing. Was he dreaming, or was that an enchanting voice he heard?

"Rex. Are you awake? How do you feel?"

It was Molly.

"Never better," he whispered.

"I'll get the doctor. Do you remember anything? You were shot saving Arthur Rugula. You were so brave, my sweet Rex." Molly pressed the call button for a nurse. Turning back to Rex and placing a hand on his arm, she rambled from topic to topic. Despite her efforts, she couldn't hide the concern in her voice.

All Rex heard was Molly calling him hers. He drifted back to sleep.

Later, he woke and remembered meeting Rugula in the park. And then the shooting. Molly was still beside him with a hand on his. It felt comforting.

"What happened? Is Rugula okay? Was the shooter apprehended?" he asked.

"Rugula's fine. He was treated for shock and released. I was able to talk with him. He's under police protection until this is all sorted," Molly replied. "He turned over evidence to the FBI that showed Kevin Greene was working with Colossus Chemical to illegally dispose of Defender. Arthur helped Henry Hoozer uncover the plot. When they got too close,

110

Greene staged the 'accident' that killed Hoozer and PJ Moregone's wife. Rugula was next."

"So the increased insurance coverage on Jane Moregone was just a coincidence?"

"Not exactly," continued Molly. "PJ Moregone and his wife were highly leveraged financially. Turns out, Moregone did the accounting for Soil Cycle, Inc. for extra cash. He kept a second set of books. He was also skimming money off the Hoopfest organization and other businesses in town.

"PJ Moregone was jealous of Henry Hoozer, who he thought was having an affair with his wife Jane. They were just friends, but Hoozer was using Jane to get information on her husband PJ and on Greene and SoilCycle," continued Molly. "According to Rugula, Greene was solely responsible for Hoozer and Jane Moregone's death. Greene may testify otherwise."

Just then a nurse entered the room followed by a doctor, who introduced himself to Rex as Dr. Ken Hu. As the nurse checked the IV, Dr. Hu said, "We've got you on antibiotics and pain medication. We removed a bullet from your leg and gave you a blood transfusion. The bullet shattered your tibia bone and part of your knee. We had to set your leg and replace the knee. Looks like you might've needed knee replacement surgery in a few years, anyway. This just moved up the date.

"The good news is once you've recovered, you'll be better than ever — your knee will feel ten years younger. The bad news is you won't be chasing down bad guys anytime soon," explained Dr. Hu, trying to sound light-hearted. "In the meantime, we'll do everything we can to make you comfortable."

Rex wished that included a cappuccino IV. Also, he wanted an update on the case. It would have to wait. Whether from the pain medication or a lack of caffeine, Rex just couldn't keep his eyes open.

Chapter 36

HOLY HEART POST-GAME PARTY

Sunday Morning

Rex woke the next morning to a visitor knocking at his hospital door. "Father O'Malley! Shouldn't you be at church?"

"There's still time. I'm here to make a special delivery and to see to it that you're healing. The parishioners will say a special mass for you this morning at St. Ignatius." He set a white, paper sack on the bedside table.

"Really Father, you didn't need to go to any bother," said Rex. But, when he saw what Father O'Malley pulled out of the sack, he added, "Bless you Father!"

"Gina thought you might prefer this to the hospital fare," the priest said while setting a steaming cappuccino and a biscotti in front of Rex. "God may be watching but we won't say anything to the hospital staff."

"You really ought to recommend the Pope canonize Gina," Rex suggested.

After Father O'Malley left, Rex turned on the KRUM-TV morning full-court press at Hoopfest. Once again, Molly Murrow reported from Riverfront Park, where Hoopfest had resumed after the capture of Kevin Greene and Mickey Gronk and the rescue of Mayor Sammy Prosciutto. Molly, dressed in a fetching, light blue sleeveless dress, was interviewing the mayor and Sergeant Phil O'Dendren, who wore his *Lucky Charmers* basketball jersey.

Mayor Prosciutto extolled the bravery and quick action of the Spokane Police Department in capturing the culprits and restoring order during the world's largest three-on-three basketball tournament.

"… The Spokane Police have cracked a case that stumped the Federal Bureau of Investigation for months. With the help of a local reporter, the

SPD unearthed the Defender caper. No more contaminated compost will destroy plants in parks and gardens throughout our city and around the nation," the mayor boasted. "Now that they've netted the perpetrators, we can return to the courts. In the spirit of Hoopfest — the games must go on."

Rex noticed that Mayor Prosciutto failed to mention Arthur Rugula by name. All that investigative work and Rugula was still overlooked. But, the mayor's on the rebound and back on the campaign trail, thought Rex. He should pick up a few basketball fans after the statewide media attention on the events at Hoopfest.

Already, the tournament had picked up where it had left off. Volunteers offered to cover additional shifts and more people stepped up to help get the competition back on track. Teams were advancing through the winners and losers brackets and headed toward the finals. The championship games were pushed back to late afternoon, a bit of a delay but still promising to conclude by the end of the day. Mayor Prosciutto could still brag about Spokane hosting a premier sporting event.

"Catching up on the tournament, I see," said Chief Barney Blueblood, entering the room. "How are you feeling this morning, Rex?"

"Chief?! I thought you'd be doing the interview with the mayor in Riverfront Park."

"What? And not stop by to check on Spokane's number one detective?"

"I don't know about number one detective. I was here in the hospital instead of catching Gronk and Greene. What happened? Where's Ivy? Is she okay? How about everyone else?"

"A player who makes the team great is more valuable than a great player," responded the chief. "You make our team great, Rex.

"Ivy stopped by last night and earlier this morning but you were asleep. She'll be back later. I ordered her to take the day off and get some rest," Blueblood continued. "Agent Bristol and a couple of SWAT team members took bullets, but they're okay," he said, adding that they were just down the hall from Rex.

Chief Blueblood told Rex how Ivy and O'Dendren subdued Gronk. Then Ivy, Bristol and the SWAT team captured Kevin Greene and rescued the mayor in the tunnels under the city. "You'd have been proud of your partner. Bad guys underestimate her at their own peril."

"That's for sure." Then, "Where'd the keg come from?" asked Rex, after expressing admiration as always with Ivy's ninja skills.

"The boneheaded Prosciutto brothers! There's a chute at O'Donovan's for rolling the kegs into the storage area under the pub. Sal and Frankie sent a full keg down the chute. They could have knocked out one of our team! They were lucky they hit Greene and created enough of a distraction that allowed the mayor to pull away and Ivy to jump the perp.

"Apparently, the mayor's brothers had extensive knowledge of the tunnels that they had picked up from their grandfather. The mayor was furious with their reckless stunt, but at the same time, thankful that it helped end the standoff," explained the chief.

"It does take a team to win a game," laughed Rex.

"Wish I could have seen Ivy take down Greene," he added. "She's really proven herself as a tough cop and a smart detective. I was leery about taking her on when you first assigned her as my partner, Chief, but she's a winner."

"I've been meaning to talk to you about Ivy. It might be time to promote her. What do you think? Is she ready to be a senior detective?" Blueblood asked.

"She's certainly qualified. She's proven herself on a number of cases. She's smart and tenacious. Once she latches onto a problem, she doesn't let go until she solves it.

"She'll have to decide whether or not she wants to take on the added responsibility and time." Then in a heavyhearted voice, Rex added, "This job can be rough on work-life balance. She's still young, though, and has lots of options."

"You aren't regretting your career now, are you Rex? You're Spokane's top detective. You've served our city for years. Is this about still being single? I've seen the way a certain reporter looks at you. You may be middle-aged my friend, but you're a long way from a rocking chair."

"You sound like my sister Sophie," said Rex.

"Speaking of…" said Sophie as she and her husband Nobu, brother Nick, sister Martina and Mama and Papa Begonia all filed into the room. Behind them, Ivy and Beau, Sergeant Phil O'Dendren, still in his basketball jersey, and officers Hemlock and Pine squeezed into the small hospital room.

Mama Begonia hugged Rex and kissed both his cheeks. Everyone began talking at once, asking how Rex was doing, remarking on his appearance and congratulating him on the case.

"Can't a guy have some peace and quiet?" laughed Rex.

"Sorry, old buddy," said O'Dendren. "No use trying to hide. We're all rooting for you to get back on your feet soon. The mayor wants to have a big ceremony honoring the SPD, especially you and Ivy, for rescuing him and saving Hoopfest."

"That's right. And the Federal Bureau of Investigation would also like to recognize the excellent law enforcement work of the Spokane Police Department," said Agent Bristol, who had rolled into the room in a wheelchair pushed by Agent Dyson. "I know we didn't exactly get off on the best foot, but you convinced us that the the SPD really knows how to hustle."

"Okay everyone. Say your good-byes. We need to clear the room. It's time to check Detective Begonia's vitals and let him rest before his lunch," said a young nurse as she wrapped a blood pressure cuff on Rex. The word lunch sent his pulse higher.

Ivy was the last to leave. As she did, she set a plant with silver gray, shield-like leaves on the bedside table next to his empty coffee cup. "*Begonia Rex-cultorum*. Thought you might like the company while you heal. See you back in the game soon, Boss."

Best partner ever thought Rex.

"You have such a large support group. You must be very popular," commented the young nurse as she finished checking his blood pressure and then held a digital thermometer to his forehead to take his temperature.

Rex grimaced. All the activity wore him out. After the nurse left, he fell blissfully to sleep.

When he awoke, he had another visitor. Standing in the doorway was a vision of beauty — a certain reporter with a radiant smile, twinkling gray eyes and sandy brown hair pulled back and clipped high behind her neck. In her smooth hands she held a tray with — his lunch.

"Hello handsome."

Chapter 37

EPILOGUE

Last Day of August

Summer's heat finally relented by the evening on the last day of August. Cheerful sunflowers, *Rudbeckia* and trailing emerald *Amaranthus* adorned the gazebo in Manito Park's Duncan Garden, where Spokane's garden clubs and Manito Head Gardener Tonie Fritts had decorated earlier in the day. A sweet floral scent drifted in the evening breeze. Beneath the flower-bedecked gazebo roof, Father O'Malley declared Beau Hunter and Ivy Lizei husband and wife.

Cheers erupted from the crowd gathered to witness the event — contingents from the Spokane Police and Fire departments and the Washington Fish and Wildlife Department, garden members and the Hunter, Lizei, O'Dendren, Begonia families and more. The ring bearer, Yukon, barked his approval.

Dressed in a simple, white, calf-length dress with emerald earrings and a pendant to match her eyes and set off her flaming-red hair, Ivy shed a tear of joy. Having grown up an only child, raised by her father and grandfather, she felt thankful for the abundance of family and friends surrounding her. She had a challenging career and, now, a life partner. She squeezed Beau's hand and they stepped forward to join their guests.

"Let's congratulate the couple," Rex said to his date, Molly, when he finally saw a chance to talk with Ivy and Beau. Leaning on a cane, he and Molly slowly made their way to the newlyweds. After shaking Beau's hand, Rex hugged his former partner and then stepped back. "Congratulations, Senior Detective Ivy Lizei, or should I say Hunter? I'm so proud of you, Ivy."

"Thanks, Boss. We haven't figured out the name thing yet. It was a rush to pull this wedding off before hunting season starts. Soon, Beau will be working long hours of overtime. You were right about going ahead and getting married just so we could see each other more often."

The maid of honor and Rex's sister Sophie approached. "What's this?! You took romantic advice from my big brother?" she teased while punching Rex lovingly. Beau and Ivy laughed.

Chief Blueblood, who was standing nearby and overheard, said, "Best mentor on the force."

Ivy's father, Joe Lizei, called the gathering's attention to the waning day and reminded everyone that a reception awaited at the nearby Cafe Noir, which had been rented for the occasion.

As Ivy and her beau climbed into his pickup truck, Ivy tossed her bouquet of white roses and green Bells of Ireland to the waiting crowd. When the throng of raised arms dropped, everyone glanced to see who had caught the bouquet — a smiling Molly Murrow.

ACKNOWLEDGEMENTS

It takes a team to produce a book! For all of your reading, editing, brainstorming and overall support, my deepest thanks go to the following winning roster: Linda Baldwin, Maureen Bieker, Jenny and Rob Bryant, Michelle Eames, Tonie Fitzgerald, Don and Nancy Giese, Ryan Giese, Lisa Langelier, Madonna Luers, Hal McGlathery, Annie McKinlay, Janet Newton and sports fan Ted Stetzik.

I would also like to acknowledge the many volunteers who make events like Hoopfest and garden shows happen in Spokane. The Lilac City boasts a bevy of garden clubs, writers, readers, artists, sports fans and more who pull together to put on fabulous events. In the Spirit of Hoopfest — You are inspiring!